where
we
are

Also by Alison McGhee

where
we
are

WITHDRAWN

ALISON MCGHEE

A CAITLYN DLOUHY BOOK

New York   London   Toronto   Sydney   New Delhi

An imprint of Simon & Schuster Children's Publishing Division
1230 Avenue of the Americas, New York, New York 10020
This book is a work of fiction. Any references to historical events, real
people, or real places are used fictitiously. Other names, characters, places,
and events are products of the author's imagination, and any resemblance
to actual events or places or persons, living or dead, is entirely coincidental.
Text © 2020 by Alison McGhee
Jacket illustrations © 2020 by photograph of girl (silhouette) copyright
grynold/Essentials collection/iStock; of boy (silhouette) copyright
Snap2Art_RF/Essentials collection/iStock; and of map courtesy
ontheworldmap.com
Jacket design by Sonia Chaghatzbanian © 2020 by Simon & Schuster, Inc.
All rights reserved, including the right of reproduction in whole or in part
in any form.
Atheneum logo is a trademark of Simon & Schuster, Inc.
For information about special discounts for bulk purchases, please
contact Simon & Schuster Special Sales at 1-866-506-1949 or business@
simonandschuster.com.
The Simon & Schuster Speakers Bureau can bring authors to your live
event. For more information or to book an event, contact the Simon &
Schuster Speakers Bureau at 1-866-248-3049 or visit our website at
www.simonspeakers.com.
Interior design by Irene Metaxatos
The text for this book was set in ITC Galliard Std.
Manufactured in the United States of America
First Edition
10 9 8 7 6 5 4 3 2 1
Library of Congress Cataloging-in-Publication Data
Names: McGhee, Alison, 1960– author.
Title: Where we are / Alison McGhee.
Description: First edition. | New York : Atheneum, [2020] | "A Caitlyn
Dlouhy Book." | Audience: Ages 14 up. | Audience: Grades 10–12. |
Summary: Told in the voices of two high school juniors, Micah is held
captive by the cult his parents joined and Sesame, his orphaned girlfriend,
rallies their friends to save him.
Identifiers: LCCN 2020018015 (print) | LCCN 2020018016 (eBook) |
ISBN 9781534446120 (hardcover) | ISBN 9781534446144 (eBook)
Subjects: CYAC: Cults—Fiction. | Missing children—Fiction. | Orphans—
Fiction.
Classification: LCC PZ7.M4784675 Wl 2020 (print) |
LCC PZ7.M4784675 (eBook) | DDC [Fic]—dc23
LC record available at https://lccn.loc.gov/2020018015
LC ebook record available at https://lccn.loc.gov/2020018016

To Aria Williams Dominguez

where
we
are

How it happened:

Because they're my parents. Because I love them. Because I worried about them. Because I thought if I stayed with them, I could keep them safe. Imagine yourself in my situation, an only child of two parents who had always adored me and worried about me and tried to keep me safe. That was our family.

Let me try this again. How It Happens.

How it happens is confusing.

Maybe I'm the thing that's confused. My mind feels kind of faded.

Try this. Look around you and state something that's

objectively true. I don't know where you are, but maybe it's hot and humid there. Maybe it's the hottest, most humid day of the summer. Say "It's hot and humid out today," which is true, right?

Now make yourself alter it. Just a little, like this, and say it in your mind. *It's hot and dry today.*

Now say it out loud. "Jeez, it's hot and dry today."

Tell yourself it's hot, which it is, and dry, which it isn't. Make yourself say it as if it's true. Torque your brain. Squeeze it. Put a little crimp somewhere inside your own maze of neurons and synapses. Then crimp the hell out of it. Go against your own self and what your own self knows to be true. *It's hot and dry today, Micah. It's hot hot hot and dry dry dry.* Tell yourself you're not sweating. Tell yourself your T-shirt isn't clammy and damp and sticking to your back, your lungs aren't filling with steamy air. Tell yourself it's too dry out for that shit.

Over and over and over, tell yourself things that aren't true, that you know *in your body* aren't true, and see what happens to you. Maybe you think you won't be able to convince yourself that something you know is true, isn't. Maybe you think you're impervious to that kind of thing.

Maybe, whoever you are and wherever you're standing on the hottest, stickiest day of the year with your clothes drenched in sweat, you're thinking something like *Whoever believes it's not humid out when it's the stickiest fucking day of the whole summer and every single woman man child dog cat bird you see is half-dead from humidity is someone who's not in control of their own senses.*

Then welcome to the South Compound.

That is how it happens.

1

Micah

WHEN THE KNOCK came, my parents were upstairs getting ready for bed, so I answered the door. It was weird to see Deeson, the head acolyte, outside of Reflection. Weirder yet to see him in a black hoodie. Not the type, Deeson. In fact, the complete opposite of a black hoodie type is Deeson. I mean, he'd tied the hoodie strings underneath his chin. But still, there he was, white face tilted up beneath the hood, appraising me.

"Bless the child, Acolyte Deeson," I said. That was— *is*—how members of the Living Lights greet each other.

"Gather your parents and your duffels and follow me," he said. "We are called to the South Compound."

See how he didn't address me as Acolyte Stone? That's Deeson. He has dead eyes. The Prophet once praised Deeson's eyes in Reflection, saying that they revealed purity of purpose. What purpose, though? That's what I wanted to ask but didn't. Like everyone else, I didn't ask questions during Reflection. One day into our underground life, I think about that. How none of us questioned the Prophet or anything he said.

Our duffels were prepacked and waiting at the top of the stairs: the white robes and white underwear we had all been issued months before, a gallon jug of water each, the Reflections book that the Prophet had written and self-published and that the Living Lights used instead of a Bible, and a brush or comb.

My parents looked up at me from the bathroom sink, where they were brushing their teeth—they always brushed their teeth at the same time—when I told them that Deeson was there, it was time to go to the South Compound, get the duffels and follow him. They didn't ask any questions. They just nodded. That's something else I think about now. They rinsed and spat and then the three of us packed our toothbrushes into our duffels and went downstairs where Deeson was waiting by the door.

"Bless the child, Acolytes Stone," he said to my parents—see, he called them acolytes—and then, "Did you send in the school excuse note last week, as instructed?"

My father nodded.

"Um, what excuse note?" I said.

"You are hereby excused from high school beginning tomorrow through the end of winter break for a family activity," Deeson said. "Fully in compliance with Minneapolis Public Schools attendance policy."

I stared at my parents, but they didn't meet my eyes. What the hell? No one had told me about this. This was a Wednesday night and there was still a week of school left before winter break began. In compliance or not, no way could I miss that much school, not junior year. And "family activity"? Deep inside me an alarm went off, an invisible, insistent alarm. Which got louder when Deeson spoke again.

"Phones," he said, and pointed at the kitchen counter.

Wait, what? Phones?

That wasn't part of Sesame's and my plan. The Prophet had been hinting that the time was nigh for the Living Lights to begin Phase Two of the project. He had bought an abandoned building somewhere in South Minneapolis— no one knew where, exactly—with the money he'd collected from the congregation, and the plan was to turn it into some kind of Living Lights Retreat Center.

Phase One: buying the building, which he named the South Compound.

Phase Two: everyone training together for retreat center life.

Phase Three: opening the retreat center.

Phase Four: Taking over the world? Making the Prophet the divine ruler of all? Shit, I don't know. I quit listening about five minutes into every one of his lectures.

Anyway.

Sesame's and my plan if they actually came for us: I would bring my phone and text her once we got to the South Compound and I knew for sure where we were.

So the phones moment was the first moment that I felt uneasy. Truly uneasy, I mean, not laugh-about-the-doings-of-the-Living-Lights-with-Sesame uneasy, not this'll-be-a-great-story-someday uneasy. Without my phone, a way to keep it charged, and enough of a signal, I would be alone, no way to contact Ses or anyone. Why hadn't we thought of that? Why hadn't we thought things through? Why hadn't we taken things seriously?

Correction: Why hadn't *I* taken things seriously?

Sesame had, from the start.

The Hello Kitty notebook that Vong, the second grader she tutors at Greenway Elementary, gave me was in my duffel. So was the matching Hello Kitty pencil, which Vong also gave me. Those things I had hidden at the bottom, wrapped inside one of the white robes. Call me prescient or call me dumb lucky, but the notebook was there. Maybe I could write to Ses, a note on notebook paper, from wherever we were going. But how would she get it? I don't have a stamp and she doesn't have a mailing address, and even though the Jameses would give it to her if I sent it to them, I don't know their address.

Hey, Ses. Can you hear me? Can you read me, coming at you from here in the laundry room of the South Compound, where I have been placed in detention? Yeah, that's right. Day one and I'm already in detention. I'm sitting in the corner, avoiding dripping white robes and writing in Hello Kitty.

Last night Deeson opened the door of our house, looked both ways, and motioned us out. My dad turned down the thermostat before leaving, which made the silent alarm inside me go off yet again. Deeson took the key from my mother's hand and locked the front door. I thought fast. Fast born of fear. Or dread, is a more accurate word. The sight of our three phones lying together on the counter next to the toaster, little rectangular corpses, panicked me. Out into the frigid December night we went. The Prophet's white passenger van was pulled up to the curb. No one was out. Why would they be? Even dogs don't want to be outside on a night like that.

"Acolyte Deeson, hold up," I said. "I have to go to the bathroom."

My parents were getting into the van, duffels over their shoulders. A hand came forward and took my mom's duffel from her. It was impossible to see more than shadows in the dark interior, but it was clear that other members of the Living Lights were already in there.

"The South Compound is nearby," he said. "You can hold it."

"I don't think I can, though," I said, and I shifted my weight from one leg to the other the way little kids do. "It's bad."

He frowned but gave me the key and jerked his thumb

toward our front door, and I ran back in. Grabbed my phone and shoved it down my underwear and then, just in case, wrote a note in dry-erase on the whiteboard for Sesame, because being Ses, she would come by as soon as she figured out I was gone.

> Hello Kitty,
> Please be on the lookout for my GPS. I think it's somewhere in the neighborhood.
> XO

Then I ran back out without peeing. Which actually I did have to, but too late now. Deeson was waiting for me outside the door, that Deeson look in his eyes. He held up his hands like he was surrendering, which was weird, but then he started patting me up and down like I'd set off an alarm at airport security. Shit. He didn't even hesitate when he got to my crotch. Fuck you, Deeson.

"Remove the phone," he said, a triumphant sound in his voice.

"I need it, though," I said, "for . . . homework. Writing papers. I can't get behind, it's my junior year."

Like somehow "junior year," that important pre-college-application year, would mean anything to him.

"Remove the phone or I will remove it for you," Deeson said.

He made me bring it back into the house, watched as

I put it back on the counter next to my parents' phones, then took the key after I locked up again. My parents were sitting on a bench in the van—it had bench seats, like pews in a church, homemade—and I squeezed in next to them, against the side. They gave me a silent, disapproving look. There were others all around us, but no one in the van said a word. Deeson was up front, driving, and as he pulled away from the curb, a panel slid down from the ceiling and closed us all in. It was dark, Ses, darker than the darkest of dark winter nights in your house.

We drove.

We drove, and drove, and drove, and it must have been hours, because I fell asleep against the cold steel wall of the van. I fell asleep and then jerked awake, fell asleep and jerked awake. I had to pee so bad. Deeson was lying when he said the South Compound was close by. The Prophet was lying when he said he'd bought an abandoned building in South Minneapolis. We are nowhere near South Minneapolis. My message on the whiteboard doesn't make any sense now.

I don't know where we are.

I don't know where we are, Sesame.

Have you been to the house yet? Did you figure out right away that the time had come and that I was gone? Did you remember where the fake rock is hidden? Was it covered with snow?

I can't send you my coordinates, Sesame, because I don't know where I am.

I screwed up, Ses. Big-time.

I got sucked into something bigger than I ever thought it could be and now I'm stuck. Here in the laundry room. Where I am temporarily "detained." My attempt to bring the phone was an infraction, which is a thing here, and the laundry room is the punishment. There's a wire screen near the ceiling, which is low, and it leads into a dark space. Maybe it's a crawl space. I can't tell. But it must be close to the outside, because last night when I couldn't sleep I heard faint sounds from the outside world. Sirens once in a while, police or ambulance, I can't tell. Every once in a while, the bark of a dog. So I know that the outside world is still there.

2

Sesame

"WHAT'S UP, SHAOLIN?" Sebastian says when I walk into the library conference room. "Why the SOS?"

Inky frowns.

"Stop," she says. "Shit's real, Sebastian."

One look at me and Inky knows. That's the thing about real friends. You don't have to say much. They know how to use those early human survival-honed instincts of categorization for purposes of good. They use them to read you—the real you, the *actual* you—and they know what's up just by the way you walk into the Walker Library conference room. Southwest High School is out for the day, and Sebastian and Inky both work evening shifts. I go to

New World Online Academy, which is a school without walls, so afternoon is our usual time to meet up.

"I know," Sebastian says. "But when shit gets real is when the monks of the Shaolin Temple find their greatest power."

He raises his hands in a prayer motion and rests his forefingers on his forehead, like some bastardized version of a yoga pose. He loves the Shaolin monks. He studies them on YouTube, their routines, their Shaolin kung fu, their food, in the same way Micah studies fire spinning. Sebastian is vegetarian because the monks are vegetarian. When he was little, his mother bought him a miniature orange robe, like monk children wear. It's pinned on his bedroom wall like a piece of art.

"Now is the time for our own Shaolin to find her innermost resources and channel them," he says, and Inky flashes out her hand and whacks him on the chest. "Jesus, Inky, what the hell?"

"Shut up," she says.

"You two," I say. "Stop. Micah's gone. He was supposed to show up last night and he didn't."

"He didn't text?" Sebastian says, and I shake my head.

"He's in trouble," I add. "I can feel it."

At that they sit up straight and their eyes turn watchful. Inky and Sebastian don't know Micah well, but they have seen me have premonitions before and they have seen those premonitions come true. They were with me two years ago, right here in this conference room, when my phone flashed an incoming call. They watched my face freeze before I even answered it, and they watched me listen to the person on the other end tell me that my grandma had collapsed and was in the hospital. They wrapped their arms around me and we triplet-walked out of the conference room and out of the library, onto Hennepin and across the street to the transit station. They jammed onto either side of me on the bus, each of them holding one of my hands.

And they stood on either side of me at the memorial service. That's what they told me later, anyway. The service is kind of a blur in my mind.

"Okay," Inky says now. "What do we do first?"

"File a missing person report," I say.

"Doesn't the person have to be missing for at least twenty-four hours before you can do that?" she says.

"Last night to now is almost twenty-four hours."

"Have you tried his parents?" Sebastian says, and I nod.

"I called their cell phones, but they went to voice mail."

"Have you called Southwest?"

"Yes. No answer. I'll try again tomorrow."

Even though the high school probably wouldn't tell me anything. Privacy rules, et cetera.

"I'll check with the office too," Sebastian says, reading my mind. "See if I can dig up any information."

Everyone loves Sebastian, especially people old enough to be his mother, which is most of the people who work at Southwest. They'd for sure respond better to him in person than to my anonymous voice on the phone inquiring after one of their students.

"And you're *sure* something's wrong?" Inky says. "You're sure they didn't just . . . go away early for winter break or something?"

"I'm sure. Micah would have told me."

Here's the thing: Micah's parents quit their jobs six months ago. They sold their car. This was the initial phase of the Prophet's "Living Lights" plan, in which all the congregants pooled their money for the betterment of the "community," quotation marks intentional. Micah was supposed to come over last night after his parents were asleep, but he didn't. I fell asleep with my phone in my hand, waiting for a text. When I woke up to nothing, no text, no call, no Micah, I knew something was wrong. It had to be the Prophet, who'd been threatening retreat to the South Compound for months now, saying it was time for Phase Two of the project, et cetera. I didn't want to call the police—I hate drawing attention to myself—but I would. For Micah, I would.

"Where do you think he is?" Sebastian says, and we both just look at him. "Don't give me your death stare. What I mean is, do you have any idea where they might have gone? Did the Prophet ever drop any hints as to where the South Compound is?"

I try to gather my thoughts. Take a deep breath and let it out slow. Keep the panic at bay.

"According to Micah, it's supposed to be an abandoned building somewhere in South Minneapolis," I say. "The Prophet bought it with the money everyone gave him. He wants to use it for the Living Lights Project."

"Which is what, exactly?"

"Some kind of business where they offer weeklong retreats designed to retrain your thinking. That's how he describes it, anyway."

"That sounds . . . weird," Inky says, after a pause. "I mean, retraining your thinking? Isn't that kind of like, um, brainwashing?"

I nod. Brainwashing fits. So does mind control.

"Who would sign up for something like that?" Sebastian asks.

"Micah's parents and a bunch of others did. My guess is that once the Prophet has them all under his control, he'll use them as free labor while he collects the money. That's the way a lot of cults operate."

"What are you, our resident cult expert?" Sebastian sounds skeptical.

But he doesn't know how much research I've done, ever since the Prophet started talking about the South Compound and the Living Lights Project. Inky frowns at him.

"If it's true, it's a fucked-up scheme," she says. "But kind of a smart fucked-up scheme, if you think about it."

"Smart if you're into mind control," I say.

"Why would Micah go with them, though?"

"I don't *know*," I say. Panic is rising in me again. Stop. Breathe.

"Maybe he didn't have a choice," Inky says.

The thought of which is terrifying. It's all sinking in. Micah is gone and he's in the hands of the Prophet and I have no idea where the South Compound could be and they must have taken his phone because he's not texting and he's not answering and—

"Whatever's happened, let's get going," Inky says, bringing me down to earth. "Ses, you file the missing person report. Sebastian, you check with school tomorrow."

"I'm going to make missing person flyers and put them up too," I say.

"Old-school," Inky says, nodding. "I like it. What else can we do right away?"

"How about social media?" I say.

I'm not on social media, and neither is Micah, but Inky and Sebastian are.

"You got it. Should we focus on the Twin Cities?" Inky says. "Or the whole United States?"

"Because there's a big difference," Sebastian points out helpfully.

"Sweet Jesus, Sebastian." Inky lifts her hand like she's about to pop him again, but I grab her hand and then Sebastian's before either of them can move.

"Please," I say. "Please, please, please."

When you have friends who know you the way they know me, that's all you have to say. What *please, please, please, please* means is *Don't waste time on anything, like being pissy with each other, because that won't help us find Micah.*

"Your aunt doesn't have any ideas?" Inky says, and I

automatically shake my head. Ever since my grandma died, I've been telling them I live with my aunt, who moved to Minneapolis to take care of me. After all this time of referring to my aunt this and my aunt that, it's like I actually do have one. Inky and Sebastian have never met my aunt, but I told them she's shy and anxious and doesn't want me to have guests over. That she's like my grandma that way.

They don't know that she doesn't actually exist. No one but Micah knows that.

Now that I'm finally a legal adult—my eighteenth birthday was last month—I guess I don't have to be so careful. But old habits die hard.

"I'll check his school locker, too," Sebastian says.

"Good," I say. "You do social media and Southwest, I'll do real world." Then an idea pops into my head. "I'll put the flyers in my poem boxes too. They get a lot of traffic."

The poem boxes. How to explain. After my grandmother died, I couldn't stop crying. For, like, weeks. It was poems that kept me going, partly anyway, poems by Ada Limón and Mary Oliver and Danez Smith and Yeats and Warsan Shire and Ocean Vuong and a hundred others. Poems about fearlessness and grief and love and loss. I used to read them to myself late at night when I couldn't sleep. And then I started memorizing them, and then I thought, *Maybe there are others out there who feel like crying all the time too*, and that's when I started the poem boxes. And I got a little obsessive about it, so it kind of turned into this project—Micah and I call it the Poetry Project.

So far it consists of wooden poem boxes that I built and mounted on trees here and there in South Minneapolis, with old Scrabble tiles glued on them that spell out FREE POEMS! HELP YOURSELF! The more poem boxes I put up, the less I cried. Now I print out my favorite poems at the library, and then I scroll them up and put them in the boxes. You'd be surprised how many people need poems, at least judging by how often I have to fill the boxes. It's like a tiny unpaid part-time job on top of my other paid part-time jobs.

"Should we see if we can find out who Micah's relatives are and contact them," Sebastian says, "on the off chance they, like, moved or something?"

"Their only relatives are distant cousins of his dad who live in Hong Kong," I say. "Micah's never even met them. His mom was an only child too, and her parents died before Micah was born. So there's no one."

They raise their eyebrows, like it's hard to believe someone can have no relatives. Maybe because Inky and Sebastian *do* have relatives. Aunts and uncles and grandparents and cousins, all of whom live nearby, so that every holiday means a big packed house full of noise and food. Micah's family isn't like that, and neither is mine. The only person I had was my grandmother, and she was suspicious of other people. Wary. She taught me to be that way too. *Be vigilant,* she used to tell me. *If you want something changed, change it yourself. Depend only on yourself. Don't ask for help.*

"Ses," Sebastian says, "are you really sure that—" But I break in before he can finish.

"Listen to me," I say. "They *didn't move.* They've been hijacked. They're in a compound somewhere here in Minneapolis with a bunch of other followers under the leadership of a madman."

They stare at me. Something in my voice, maybe. Hearing myself say it out loud like that makes it sound crazy, which it is. Why didn't I take it more seriously? Why didn't I make Micah take it more seriously? It was so ridiculous—a cult? I mean, come on—but sometimes things start ridiculous and then turn dangerous. Somebody like my grandmother would have seen that from the start. *Watch out, girl,* she would have said. *Tread carefully.*

"But—wasn't Micah kind of going along with this whole thing, though? I don't remember him being too worried," Sebastian says, after a moment. "I mean, he used to laugh when he talked about how boring the Prophet was and how he could hardly stay awake during his lectures."

Like he's trying to make it sound not-bad, almost like a boring high school class.

"He *was* worried," I say. "He was just trying to minimize the creepiness of his parents joining a cult."

"Why would he go with them, then?"

"Maybe he didn't have a choice. Or maybe he was trying to keep an eye on them. Protect them."

"That's so warped," Inky says. "I mean, parents are supposed to protect *us,* not the other way around."

"Yeah. But it doesn't always happen that way. Listen, will you do something with me? Like, right now?" I say, and they nod.

"Anything," Inky says, and "Of course," Sebastian says. "What?"

"Come with me to his house."

Micah's house is small and stucco, painted bright green, on the north end of the alley between Garfield and Harriet. Micah grew up with the sound of cars turning into or out of the alley all day and much of the night, heading for their garages. My house is on an alley too. It's one of the things we both love, that sound of tires crunching on snow or humming on asphalt. We love winter, too. Sometimes when we're alone I quote him a poem I love by Mike White, "Alley in Winter," about how beautiful the fire escape is, all coated in ice, after a fire. That's the thing about living in a place like Minneapolis. You learn to see a different kind of beautiful, the beautiful that happens after something ordinary, like water, transforms itself into something dazzling.

"Are we going to have to break in?" Sebastian says, once we're at the front door.

He likes the idea of that. You can tell. He's already swiveling his head, looking for a basement window to pry open. Or maybe he's checking for cops, because teenagers + after school + locked doors + suspicious behavior = possible cops. But I shake my head. I know where the Stones keep their key. Yeah, their last name is Stone and they named their son Micah. Not sure they knew that mica is a kind of rock.

Then again, my grandma named me Sesame. She said it was because she grew up saying, "Open, Sesame!" when she wanted something good to happen. And that adopting me was like the best thing in the world ever to happen to her.

I shake my head and start pawing through the snow to the left of the front doorsteps.

"For real?" Inky says when I pry out the fake rock and brush the snow off it. "Like nobody would ever think there was a house key hidden in there?"

Yes, the Stones keep their key in the kind of fake rock that looks entirely fake. Which when you think about it makes sense. If the Stones couldn't see how fake their fake rock is, then they wouldn't be able to tell a fake prophet from a real one either. Although, are there real prophets? Or are there just people who like to think they know more than the rest of us?

Sebastian looks disappointed. Maybe he's bummed we aren't going to have to break into the house. Or maybe he's having the same fake rock thought that I am. I unlock the door with the frozen key and swing it open. Inside, it's still and cold and empty. You can always tell when a house is uninhabited. Don't ask me how I know this. I'll tell you another time. But it's true. I check the thermostat by the door. It's turned to fifty-five, which is something you do only if you're not going to be around for a while. Minneapolis in December is not a fifty-five-degree-thermostat kind of place. The living room is spotless, as if company's coming.

In the kitchen, I open the refrigerator, and everything inside is Micah. Clear glass containers labeled and dated: spinach lasagna and spareribs and pound cake and chicken noodle soup and kimchee and roasted beets. There is nothing Micah can't cook. Cooking is what he does for the people he loves, like his parents. Like me.

The sight of Micah's food in this Micah-less house twists something inside me, something new—worry over him—and something old, which is missing my grandmother. She used to cook for me too. I shut the refrigerator door and start to head upstairs, and that's when I see the phones.

Three little phones, side by side next to the toaster.

His dad's phone in its red case. His mom's in blue.

And Micah's, in the silver case I gave him last Christmas.

So. They're gone for real.

"What?" Sebastian says as I stand there frozen, staring at the phones. "What is it?"

Then he and Inky both see them too. "Shit," Inky says.

My heart is pounding, but I make myself go upstairs, and they follow. Towels are hung over the shower rod to dry, but no toothbrushes are in the SpongeBob SquarePants toothbrush holder. No toothpaste on the sink.

I think for a minute.

The call must have come quickly. Not enough time to put the leftovers in the freezer so they'd last, but enough time to shove a toothbrush in a bag. Enough time to be told to leave their phones on the counter. We go back downstairs. At the sight of the phones, lined up so neatly on the counter by the toaster, my stomach clenches. I pick up Micah's phone—it's cold, like everything else in this house—and cradle it in both my hands. It's not dead yet. I open it with his passcode, which I know by heart, and flick to the texts.

The last one from me: k see you soon ☺

Flick to the calls: nothing.

E-mails: only one unread one, some mass mailing from Southwest High School about the upcoming winter break.

"You think the prophet guy made them leave their phones behind?" Sebastian says.

"Of course, dumb-ass," Inky says. "Nobody just leaves their phones behind like that."

Their voices fade into the background. Micah's trapped somewhere and he doesn't have his phone. My heart is still racing. It makes me crazy, knowing he's out there somewhere but I have no way of knowing where and no way of reaching him. Panic. *Breathe,* I tell myself, but it doesn't help. Then I notice the whiteboard by the back door, the one that the Stones leave messages for each other on. There's only one message now, in black dry-erase pen, in Micah's spiky printing.

Hello Kitty,
Please be on the lookout for my
GPS. I think it's somewhere in the
neighborhood.
     XO

"That's from Micah," I say, pointing. My voice is tiny. Not like me. When did he write this? Did they see him write it? "It's a message for me."

"He calls you Kitty?" Inky says. "That's weird."

"No, it means he brought the Hello Kitty notebook with him. Vong gave it to him. And the GPS thing must mean I should look for him. He knew I'd come over here eventually and see the message."

"It's really cold in here," Sebastian says. "It feels abandoned."

"It *is* abandoned, dumb-ass," Inky says. Inky doesn't have a lot of patience. She turns to me. "Should we ask the neighbors if they noticed anything?"

But I don't know the neighbors, and anyway, a little house on the edge of an alley doesn't have neighbors the way a house in the middle of the block has neighbors, and anyway more, I don't like talking to people I don't know well. That's a holdover life lesson from my grandmother. So I shake my head. Sebastian and Inky leave by the back door, the one that gives directly onto the garbage and recycling cans, so they can see if anything's out of place there, and I lock up and rebury the fake rock in the snow.

I'm smoothing the snow so it looks undisturbed when I get a text. It's from James One.

Sesame G, it's James One.

So formal. Like I don't already know it's him from my contact info? But James One always begins texts that way, as if he's leaving a voice mail.

The office closed early today, so I'm home with the dogs and will walk them. You have the day off!

Relief wells up in me—I can file the missing person report right away—mixed with worry, because days off mean no pay. James One is still writing, though.

You will of course be paid for the whole week as usual. See you tomorrow!

I should have known. The Jameses would never try to stiff me. I'm pretty sure even my wary grandmother would've eventually given in to the charm, respectability, and kindness of the Jameses.

Every weekday, rain or shine or sleet or snow, the mail carriers are out carrying mail and I'm out walking my dogs. They're not *my* dogs—they belong to the Jameses—but I think of them as mine. I've been walking them every day while the Jameses are at work, and on some weekends, too, ever since my grandma died. Orphans have to earn their full living. Orphans have to find a place to live. Orphans have to stay vigilant, change the things they need changed, protect themselves, and not ask for help.

Sebastian and Inky have never seen my house. They don't even know where it is.

No one knows where my house is except for Micah. Somehow the thought that no one knows where I live except him brings it flooding over me. I'm alone. Micah's gone. My grandma's gone. I'm alone. Oh my God. Oh my God.

"I don't have to walk the pups today," I say, trying to make my voice sound normal. "I can head straight to the police."

"You want us to come with?" Inky says—she can tell how shaky I am right now—and Sebastian nods, like he's okay with that idea.

I would actually love them to come with me, but I know Inky has a shift at Spyhouse Coffee and Sebastian's due at Kowalski's, so, no. I shake my head.

"I'll handle that. You two plaster his photo on social media," I say. "And if anyone responds, or anything else occurs to you, like, anything at all, text me, okay?"

"Will do, Shaolin," Sebastian says. "Meanwhile, see you tomorrow. Same time, same place."

He makes his prayer hands/yoga/namaste/praying monk signal again. Inky doesn't say anything. She gives me an Inky hug, which means that it lasts a long time. She read an article once that said that you don't get the true benefit of a hug unless it lasts at least six seconds, and ever since then Inky's hugs have been the longest, tightest, and best. Except for Micah's.

3

Micah

SESAME, REMEMBER THE day Vong gave me the Hello Kitty notebook? I waited for you in the office—the tutoring room at Greenway Elementary is connected to it—with a cappuccino for you and animal crackers for Vong, just in case he came trailing after you, like usual. Which he did.

"Thanks, mate," Vong said, as if he were British.

"Anytime, old chap."

Might as well play along with the British thing, right? He dug around in his backpack and hauled out a Hello Kitty notebook and matching pencil.

"This is a present for you, Micah," he said.

A Hello Kitty notebook? Was he joking or was he for

real? With Vong it's hard to tell. Either way, I didn't want to hurt his feelings, so I smiled and said thanks.

"Use it for the forces of good," Vong said. "Not evil."

Remember how we looked at each other, Ses? Both making a silent pact not to laugh, which is often the way it is around Vong. Such a funny and solemn little kid, with his chopped-off hair and random fake British accents and strange commands. I nodded.

"Also," he said, "there's a poem in it."

I opened the notebook while he watched.

> Roses are red
> Violets are blue
> Someday I'll write a poem TOO.

"Nice," I said. "Tell you what, maybe I will too."

Vong inclined his head. "P'raps."

Weird that he has a hard time reading and writing, when his speech and vocabulary are so good. You told me he won't open his mouth in the classroom, which is how he originally got signed up for before-school tutoring. But when he's around you, he never shuts up. The thing is, though, it's like Vong actually gave Hello Kitty special powers when he told me to use it for forces of good, because that same day, I started carrying that notebook in my own backpack. Started making sketches and notes in it, ideas for the future. Hello Kitty holds all our plans for the future, Ses.

Our future ice sculpture for the luminaria on Lake of the Isles in February.

Our future fire spinner routines.

Our future around-the-world couch-surfing travels. I want to start from the Pacific and you want to start from the Atlantic, but whatever.

And our future café right here in Minneapolis.

Hello Kitty holds all kinds of secret plans, all written down with the Hello Kitty pencil. They're both here with me in the South Compound. Deeson and the Prophet don't know I have them.

Which is a good thing, what with the phone infraction. When we get out of here, when things are back to normal, I'll show it to you. For now I'm just keeping coded notes in it about life down here. Scraps of information, like the coded note I left you on the whiteboard. Once things are back to normal and the Prophet's back to being the ordinary loser he was born to be, you and I will look at the coded notes and laugh. *When things are back to normal.* I keep using that phrase, don't I?

It's weird being down here, Sesame.

I listen as hard as I can, and what I hear are the sounds of whatever city they drove us to, coming in faintly through the vent or whatever it is, up there on the laundry room wall. If we were in the country, there'd be no sounds, right? Or there would be unfamiliar sounds, like tractors and roosters, maybe. Maybe coyotes howling in the middle of the night? I don't know. I'm a city person, not a country person.

Ses, remember how in the beginning I used to tell you not to call them the Lightlys? Because it made them sound like a cult, and I hated the idea of my parents being in a cult? You were right, though. The Prophet is actually saying the end is nigh, just like in all the cartoons. It's funny except not, because he means the end of life as we know it, life in the secular world. "Abandonment of the secular world is now, for the end of life in darkness is nigh, and the beginning of life in light is nigh, and . . ." Nigh nigh nigh blah blah blah.

Everyone listens to him. How did I not notice that before, how seriously everyone takes him? I'm the only one who laughs. And only on the inside. Because if I actually laugh, which I did the first time he said it, the consequences will be "severe."

Remember when you asked how my parents got mixed up with him? And I didn't go into details because it makes them look so . . . dumb? That's because it *is* dumb.

I still can't wrap my head around it. I mean, my parents were ordinary people until my thirteenth birthday, which is when the Prophet knocked on the door in the middle of everyone singing happy birthday to me. Cake. Candles. Pile of presents, which at the time were all related to phosphorescence, which was the topic of the year for me when I was thirteen. A book on photochemistry, a tiny mechanical jumping firefly made by a company in Germany, a Christmas tree ornament in the shape of a firefly, a cake in the shape of a firefly. All things firefly.

Feels like a long time ago now.

Then came the knock at the door. There was something strange about the knock. I can still hear it in my head. It wasn't a two- or three-rap knock, it was five sharp raps separated by a second or so each. *Rap. Rap. Rap. Rap. Rap.*

Who would answer the door to a weird knock in the middle of your son's firefly birthday celebration? No one. My dad did, though. He opened up the door like he was expecting guests, and there they were: the Prophet and two of his acolytes. Yes, that was what he called them, even back then.

"Good evening," he said. "My acolytes and I are here on behalf of an educational group designed to help cope with the rigors of modern-day life. It's called Living Lights. Are you interested in learning more about our program?"

Such weird formal language, along with those cold eyes of his. I waited for my parents to politely say no and shut the door, which was what they did with everyone else who came door-knocking. But they didn't. They let him in.

Let's make a shitty movie about a religious cult that uses every stereotype possible. Take an aging male Prophet with creepy eyes. Dress him in a white robe. Surround him with submissive acolytes also wearing white robes. Have them go door-to-door recruiting new members of their cult. Have Deeson, the head acolyte, and his wife stand on street corners downtown with signs that read ABANDON THE SECULAR WORLD and give out brochures about the Living Lights Project. At some point, have them all, at a predetermined signal from the Prophet, descend into the secret South Compound for Phase Two of the project, which consists of . . . oh yeah, abandonment of the secular world. Which is what we're doing down here, according to the Prophet. After which we will all emerge cleansed and ready to carry out Phase Three of the project, which is to establish the Living Lights Retreat Center.

Shit. I guess I *have* been listening.

"What is the important work we are engaged in, acolytes?" the Prophet says at the beginning of Reflection.

"Abandonment of the secular world, Prophet," everyone but me answers back. I mouth the words, but I don't actually say them.

This is the way they're talking, down here in the South Compound. Even my parents. My parents, who for whatever reason decided to let the Prophet into our lives. You want to know the truth? I wish I was standing on a sidewalk holding a sign that reads ABANDON THE SECULAR WORLD. Because then I wouldn't be down here. I'd still be in the world, and I'd run away.

There are seventeen members of the Living Lights Project, plus the Prophet.

Fallon and Gregory M. and their three children, Jonathan, Jerald, and Jerralyn. Each of the J children—I can't keep them straight—is approximately the same size and has dark hair in a bowl cut. In their white robes, I literally forget who's who.

Karenne and Jacob P. and their daughter, Krystyna.

Krystyna used to spell her name Christina, but she changed it in fifth grade because another girl in her class was named Christina, and the other Christina was mean and Krystyna wanted to set herself apart from the mean Christina. She told me this in a whisper before Reflection this morning. The Prophet saw her talking to me and told her to sit up front and not speak to me again. I had to restrain myself from telling him that Krystyna hadn't been *speaking*, she'd been *whispering*. I don't want to be locked in the laundry room again.

Andrea K., her husband, Jack S., and their twin daughters, Sarena and Liliane. Sarena is half an inch taller than Liliane, and she lets everyone know it. She did, anyway, until the Prophet overheard her and told her that boasting was one of the seven deadly sins. Which, do you mean "pride," Prophet? Anyway, she's six years old, Prophet. Pretty sure that six-year-olds are exempt from the deadly-sin stuff. Or they should be.

Sandra and Rick Stone and their son, Micah.

Deeson and a small, scared-looking woman who must be his wife because that's what he calls her: Wife.

And of course, the Prophet.

The Prophet and Deeson must have figured everything out before they brought everyone down here, because they started right in with a rigid daily schedule. We are in a basement of some kind, a huge one with various rooms, each with a different function: Room of Sleeping, Room of Eating, Room of Food Preparation, Room of Reflection,

Room of Laundry, and Bathroom. The bathrooms are the only rooms with a normal name. Not sure what you'd call them otherwise—Room of Bath? Room of Toilet? Room of Sink, Toilet, and Shower?

A chore chart is thumbtacked to the dining room wall, listing everyone's names and assigned chores.

Reflection and Self-Examination are not on the chore chart, because it's expected that everyone will participate in both.

Scrub bathrooms: Jerald and Liliane
Wash dishes: Krystyna and Jerralyn
Meal prep: Karenne and Jack
Meal serving: Andrea K. and Wife
Sweeping: Sandra and Sarena
Dusting: Gregory and Jonathan
Whitewashing: Fallon and Rick and Jacob
Laundry: Micah

Each bathroom—one for the males and one for the females—has two toilets and two sinks. The dining table seats nine, which means two sittings for each meal. The dishes have to be washed in cold water because there's no hot. Whitewashing . . . what even is whitewashing? Well, let me tell you. Whitewashing means painting the walls of each room white. Every single room, white. Ceilings and floors and hallways, too. Yeah.

Everything that comes out of the kitchen is white as

well: white potatoes, white bread, white mayonnaise, white chicken, white milk. I don't trust food that has no color.

Laundry is my chore. Everyone wears white robes and white underwear and white socks, and guess who gets to wash it all? By hand? With a washboard and two laundry tubs? Yeah.

Micah Stone Point System: Apparently Deeson and the Prophet suspected I would be trouble from the start, because I was given one hundred points to begin with, and with every infraction, points are deducted. It's like a kindergarten star chart, which would be funny if it were funny, which it isn't. Deeson and the Prophet must have dreamed the Micah Stone point system up early, before we ever got here, because a chart already pinned to the door of the Room of Reflection lists all the possible Micah Stone infractions and how many points for each.

Insubordination: 5
Poor Work Ethic: 5
Adherence to the Secular World: 5

I began with a hundred points and already I'm down to ninety because I didn't get the robes white enough (Poor Work Ethic) and I didn't pay close enough attention in Reflection (Adherence to the Secular World). With regard to my infractions, I say: You ever tried washing a dirty white cotton robe by hand in cold water? You ever try sitting through one of the Prophet's lectures?

No one else has a points chart. No one else has a list of possible infractions.

They are using me as an example for the children. Jonathan, Jerald, Jerralyn, Krystyna, Sarena, and Liliane are studying me in Living Lights, as an example of the opposite of Living Lights. Micah Stone lacks self-awareness. Micah Stone has a poor work ethic. Micah Stone is at high risk of insubordination. Micah Stone clings to the secular world.

Sesame, did you find the note I left you?

Do you know where I am?

Because I don't.

Sesame

AFTER INKY and Sebastian and I leave Micah's house, I head straight to the Fifth Precinct. I don't know if you can file a missing person report over the phone—I've never filed one before—but it doesn't seem right. No way can an officer come to my house, and if I have anything to do with it, no one will. So I walk from Uptown over to the Fifth Precinct office on Nicollet, next to the bus garage. Inside, it looks just like a television police department. Fluorescent lights, banged-up utilitarian desks, tired-looking staff.

"I'd like to file a missing person report," I say to the person behind the desk. He directs me to Officer Emmanuel, who sits me down at a desk and asks me a bunch of questions.

"What's your name and address, please?"

I give Officer Emmanuel my name—Sesame Gray—and the Jameses' address. Their address is the one I use when I need an official address, like for New World Online Academy, and for my bank card, things like that. After my grandmother died and I started living on my own, I asked the Jameses if that would be okay, because my aunt's apartment didn't have a street address, just a PO box. They didn't even blink. "Of course," they both said at the same time. "Anytime." The Jameses are trusting people.

"And who is the person you'd like to report?"

"Micah Stone. My boyfriend."

"Age and address?"

"Seventeen." I give her his address and also his parents' names, tell her that he's a junior at Southwest High School, we've been together a year and a half, no, he isn't currently working, yes, he's a full-time student. I show her some photos of him on my phone.

"He lives with his parents?"

"Yes. They're missing too."

She gives me a look, like why didn't I say that in the first place. I explain that his parents joined a cult, but Micah didn't.

"So you're saying he's with his parents right now?"

I don't like the way she asks the question. Something in her tone. Didn't she hear what I said? About his parents joining a cult?

"Yes, I think so," I say, "but the Prophet came and got them all and took them to the South Compound and made them leave their phones behind."

She takes her hands off the keyboard, sits back, and looks at me in this confused and patient way. I don't blame her. Nothing I'm saying makes much sense.

"And what's the nature of your concern, Miss Gray? Why do you think that Micah's disappeared under adverse circumstances?"

"I told you. Because his parents are in a *cult*. And the leader of it, this guy, the Prophet, has been saying that it's time for Phase Two, and that the secular world must be abandoned, and that the South Compound awaits."

Saying it out loud like that to a police officer makes it sound even crazier, like I'm reading from some B-grade movie script that no one's ever going to turn into an actual movie. She blinks but keeps her eyes on me. Maybe she's used to dealing with strangeness.

"I see. And what makes you think that now is the time?"

"Because I haven't heard from Micah, and that's totally unlike him. And Inky and Sebastian and I went to his house and the heat was turned way low and their phones were on the counter and their duffels and sleeping bags were gone. And there was a note on the whiteboard."

I tell her about the note and what I think it means, and Officer Emmanuel nods. "So in your opinion, Micah is with his parents, in a secret compound of some kind, and the compound is somewhere nearby?"

Listening to her say it like that makes me sound like I'm paranoid, delusional, but I nod anyway. "Yes," I say, with force, which makes me sound defensive in addition to paranoid.

"And he's seventeen, you say?"

"Yes. I just turned eighteen." Which, why did I say that? My eyes suddenly sting and the panic comes rushing back in. I can hear my grandmother's voice telling me to be wary. Be vigilant. Don't ask for help. *Protect yourself, Sesame. Breathe. Breathe.*

"I assume you've checked in with Micah's other friends? Checked all his social media accounts?"

"He doesn't do social media. And Inky and Sebastian are checking with his other friends at school. They all go to Southwest together."

She nods and turns back to the keyboard. She's not a bad person, Officer Emmanuel. She's patient. She's taking down the information even if it doesn't make a lot of sense. The last time I saw Micah was two days ago. No, there was no note in the house except the whiteboard message. No, Micah and his family have no relatives to contact. No, his parents don't have work contacts because they quit their jobs six months ago. Then I volunteer that my aunt's away in California for a month, taking care of her best friend who has cancer, a lie I made up on the spot but that doesn't seem to bother her. I give her the Jameses' phone numbers as emergency contacts because my aunt doesn't have a cell phone, which is another lie. My nonexistent aunt with her nonexistent phone. She asks for other contacts, both my friends and other adults so that she can follow up with them, and I give her Inky's and Sebastian's full names, along with their parents' names and addresses. Inky and Sebastian and their families are safe for Officer Emmanuel to contact. She taps away on the keyboard and then turns to me.

"Good," she says. "The more information you can gather, the better. I'll follow up with Inky and Sebastian and their parents tomorrow, and also with Southwest and the Jameses. Given that Micah and his parents have no relatives, as far as you know"—I nod—"be sure to contact anyone you can think of, anyone at all who might know where they've gone."

I wait, but she doesn't say anything else.

"That's it?" I say. "You're not going to, like, search for him?"

Which sounds so lame. Where would they search? Minneapolis is a big city.

"At this point, given everything you've told me, I am not convinced that Micah is in imminent danger. According to you, he is with his parents, and given that our records show no known history of neglect"—she must have checked Child Protective Services while we were talking—"and given that it's almost winter break, they may have decided to head out early on a family vacation."

"They didn't!" I protest. "You don't know them; they don't *do* things like that. Anymore, anyway."

"Is it a possibility, though, Miss Gray? Even a remote possibility?"

The remotest of remote possibilities, I think. But the image of it—the three of them with their duffels on a train heading somewhere for a couple of weeks—is for one second so comforting, such a contrast to the image of them descending into some doomsday dungeon somewhere, that I nod. A tiny nod.

"All right then," Officer Emmanuel says. "You were right to come in and talk to us, Miss Gray. You're a good friend, that much is obvious. I've entered the information you gave me, so the case can be made active anytime if necessary. What I want you to do is keep me posted. Do everything you can to figure out where he is, and call me immediately if you come across anything alarming."

She taps on the keyboard a little longer, closes out the screen, stands up, gives me her card and shakes my hand, then walks me to the door. A boy goes missing and this is all they can do? This is all *I* can do? I stand at the door—it's dark now, in the late afternoon—and look in the direction of home, twelve blocks from this precinct and its fluorescent lights and its officers who see no immediate cause for alarm.

"Keep the faith now," she says, and waves goodbye.

Once outside, panic overflows inside me. I don't know what to do. *I don't know what to do, I don't know what to do, I don't know what to do.* My legs start to run and they carry me along with them. Run and run and run down the icy, snowy side-walks. Run and run and run past houses covered with snow and Christmas lights, twinkling trees visible behind windows. Run and run and run past all the people who live with the people they love. Run and run and run even though my boots aren't running boots and my eyelashes are clumping up with snow. Run and run and run because Micah was supposed to come over last night and he didn't and he doesn't have his phone and he would never leave his phone he would never ever leave his phone lined up next to his parents' phones like bowls of Goldilocks oatmeal on the counter and I don't know where he is and I don't know what to do because where is he and how can I help if I don't know where he is and my gut keeps yelling that *no one will believe you no one will believe you no one will believe you*—STOP.

STOP.
STOP.
STOP.

My boots slow down and I'm walking now, not run-ning. The streets and their sidewalks come back into focus. *It'll be okay, Sesame. It'll be okay, Sesame. You'll figure out a way, Sesame. You'll figure out a way.* My mantras. The mantras that have gotten me through. Gotten me through, gotten me through, gotten me through all the times when I've had to take care of myself.

You'll figure it out, Sesame.

Step one: Don't panic. Panic will accomplish nothing. You can figure this out.

Step two: Know what you know. What you know is that he's gone. Don't listen to anyone who tries to tell you differently, because your gut knows what it knows.

Step three: Use all the tools at your disposal. You already filed the police report, or tried to anyway. You delegated social media to Inky and Sebastian. Now you'll make missing person flyers—photo, description, missing as of, please contact—and distribute them. You'll fill the poem boxes with flyers too. Think hard for any clues, any clues at all about the South Compound. Go back over every conversation you and Micah ever had about the Prophet, the Lightlys, and their future plans.

Step four: Go home and go through all the steps one by one. Repeat as necessary.

So home I go. My hands in mittens shoved into my jacket pockets because damn. It's cold. It's so cold. I picture Micah outside without a jacket or boots, freezing, hypothermia, frostbite, dead white feet dead white hands—NO. Don't panic. Panic will accomplish nothing.

I slip down the alley to my house. Around to the side door. Unlock it with the silver key on the leather cord. Close the door tight before I turn on the single twenty-five-watt lamp right next to my bed and my chair and my table, yes all of them at once because my house is smaller than any house you've ever seen.

Step two I can skip because I already know what I know.

Step three is me, making a missing person flyer. I sit on my bed and cut me out of the five-by-seven photo of

Micah and me that Sebastian took last summer at Lake Bde Maka Ska. The scissors curve around my shoulder, my arm, my head leaning toward his. It's awful, slicing us apart like this. When I'm done, there's Micah, his head leaning right toward an empty space, smiling at the camera. My throat is tight and hurting, but I won't cry. This is the only actual, printed photo I have of him. I tape it onto a sheet of blank paper and pick up my black Sharpie.

Missing: Micah Stone, 17

It's horrible, writing those words. I write more: date last seen, student at Southwest High School, and my cell phone number. Should I write in Inky's and Sebastian's, too? No. Keep it simple. I glance over at my phone, lying patiently on the bed. Is it charged? It's charged. I plug it in anyway. My phone needs to be fully charged at all times from here on out.

It's late. It's cold. FedEx Office is open 24/7, though, so out I go again, back into the frozen city. Five blocks to FedEx Office, next door to Lunds groceries, both of them bright and open and warm. I make two hundred color copies and oh my God! How can it possibly cost that much? I don't have this kind of money! The man behind the counter sees the panic in my eyes and asks what's wrong. That's when I start to cry. Damn it.

"Sticker shock?" he says, and I nod, like the expense of making copies is enough to make me cry.

"Tell you what," he says. "I'm knocking fifty percent off your bill. We'll chalk it up to poor-quality copies."

His kindness makes me cry harder. I thank him and push back out the door. Starting tomorrow, before and after I go tutor Vong at Greenway Elementary, I will staple these flyers to every pole in South Minneapolis and put one in every one of my poem boxes. What else can I do? What else can I do? What else what else what else—STOP.

Step one: Don't panic, Sesame. Panic will accomplish nothing. You can figure this out.

My grandmother's voice comes back to me: *If you want something changed, change it yourself.*

5

Micah

HELLO KITTY, let me tell you about the day I met Sesame. It was down an alley, not far from the Rose Garden. She didn't know anyone was watching. You could tell by how free she moved. *That girl would be a good fire spinner* was the thought I had when I saw her. Fire spinning is something I'm interested in. Later, months after that day, I pulled up some YouTube videos to show her.

"We should learn how to spin fire," I said. "Wouldn't that be a cool thing to do, like out on the ice on Lake of the Isles in the middle of winter?"

We were both leaning in over my phone. It was late at night and we were at her house. Fire dancers spun and twirled on the cracked screen while fire flickered around them. Sesame's hair was pulled back and held in place with a chopstick, which is the kind of thing she does. Twigs, chopsticks, pencils, I've seen them all in her hair.

When I saw her in the alley that first day, the first thing I thought was that she was beautiful. Not in a jump-out-at-you kind of way, but an unostentatious way. A stealth way, which made sense because most people walk down streets, not alleys. You can find cool things in alleys, though, like the mosaic mural behind the Black Forest Inn made of colored glass and broken pieces of pottery and rock that reads WHAT IS IT YOU PLAN TO DO WITH YOUR ONE WILD AND PRECIOUS LIFE?

When I told her about that mural, of course she had already seen it. She's a wander-the-alleys girl who's wandered all the alleys of South Minneapolis. She told me the mural is the ending line of a poem by Mary Oliver. Girl knows her poetry.

If you make it a habit to walk around southwest Minneapolis, you'll see traces of Sesame. You won't know it's her. All you'll know is that one day, when you decide for the hell of it to walk down an alley instead of the street-facing sidewalk, you'll come across a small wooden box with a lid, hanging off the trunk of a skinny tree, held on with a strap or a belt or a bungee. No nails, so as not to hurt the tree. The only kind of tree that grows in an alley is a scrappy tree that planted itself and grew where it wanted, with no help from anyone. Sesame's preferred kind of tree.

The box will be painted green, because green in all shades is Sesame's favorite color. Maybe you won't notice the Scrabble tiles that spell out

on the side of the box. Out of curiosity—what is this green box doing attached to this tree in this alley?—you'll lift the lid. You'll wonder what all those scrolled-up pieces of paper are. You won't see what I see in my mind, which is the table in the corner of Sesame's house covered with poems that she loves, waiting to be scrolled up. She says she walks around with poets in her head, lines from them drifting through her mind. She says she can hear them, like literally hear the poets talking to her, reciting their poems. Warsan Shire asking the world where it hurts, Lucille Clifton whispering about the time she lost a baby, Elizabeth Acevedo shouting about a rat, Michael Lee searching for his lost friend, Guante and his ten responses to the phrase "man up."

That girl lives and breathes poetry.

Maybe you'll lift out a poem and unroll it. Maybe you'll stand there, reading the poem to yourself. Maybe you'll read it out loud. If you're with someone else, maybe you'll both take another poem. Maybe you'll take three or four. Maybe you'll walk down the alley reading poems to each other.

That would make her happy. It's why she came up with the Poetry Project in the first place. "Because too many people are sad and too many people are alone," she says. Poems are a way to unlonely the lonely. And Sesame is lonely. Even though she has me, and Inky and Sebastian, Sesame knows what lonely feels like.

Up until the Day of the Alley, had anyone asked me when was the last time I saw Sesame Gray, I would have said Lake Harriet Elementary. *Yeah, I remember Sesame Gray. She rode the same bus as me. She used to get off at 31st and Lyndale. If that's the same Sesame Gray you're talking about.* Which it would've been. I mean, how many Sesame Grays do you meet in your life? I hadn't ever talked to her, back then. We weren't friends. She was a shadow in the back of the class when I thought about elementary school, a shadow on the playground, a shadow by the window in the middle of the bus.

Are you listening, Ses? Can you feel my thoughts, beaming out to you from this place where I am?

We must have crossed paths between elementary school and the Day of the Alley. We were little kids who went to the same school and rode the same bus, and after we graduated, I went to Southwest and Sesame went somewhere else. There are lots of high schools in Minneapolis and lots of private schools. There are even non-school high schools, like New World Online Academy, where Sesame goes now. New World Online Academy, the school without walls, where classes and homework are done on your own time from wherever you are. New World Online Academy is everywhere, and it's nowhere.

Kind of like Sesame herself.

If you walk the city of Minneapolis, you'll be in the presence of Sesame. You just won't know it. She's kind of like a female Banksy, the street artist, only with poems.

"You don't know Banksy's a he, Micah. Banksy could just as easily be a she. Banksy could be living in Minneapolis for all anyone really knows."

She was right. She *is* right. Stop mixing up past and present, Micah. Keep it in the present tense. Sesame is like Banksy in that she and her poem boxes are under the radar and everywhere. Everyone recognizes a Banksy when they see it, though, and no one recognizes a Sesame.

After elementary school, Sesame Gray would have faded out of my mind forever, maybe, if I hadn't turned down the alley that one day because I was bored with sidewalks. You want a change, turn down an alley instead of the sidewalk. Look at the backs of houses instead of the fronts. Look at the garages. Some will have their doors rolled up, and you'll see the things that people store inside them. Weird shit, some of it. Hoarder shit, some of it. Entirely organized and spare, some of it. You'll see the kind of people who turn their garages into workshops, who spend hours and hours in those workshops, making things. You might even see a garage that someone turned into the coolest one-room house in the world.

This is how I distract myself, Sesame. I think about you.

Are you asleep right now? I'm not, here on this cot in the closet that the Prophet has decreed my bedroom. Room of Micah. The adults are asleep down the hall in various rooms that must have at one time been offices and are now designated as separate Rooms of Sleeping for boys and girls and men and women. Micah is asleep in the janitorial supply closet labeled ROOM OF MICAH.

The closet is just big enough to fit the army cot I'm on, and the cot is barely big enough for me. If you were here we'd make room, though. We wouldn't care about the lack of space. We'd make it work. We'd listen hard for the sound of sirens wailing, like they were wailing in the distance last night. Ambulances, police cars, and the distant beeps of big trucks backing up. City sounds.

When they brought us here, we drove for I don't know how many hours. Forever and ever, we drove. I wish I hadn't left that note for you on the whiteboard. What cities are within hours—five hours, six hours?—of Minneapolis?

Des Moines.

Madison.

Sioux Falls.

Duluth.

Chicago, if you were driving fast, which I don't think we were.

Any others? What about Winnipeg? Is that close enough? Why don't I know?

Maybe I'm not as smart as I used to think. Why didn't I have a plan for if they wouldn't let us bring our phones? Was it because I didn't believe it would actually happen? Was it because I didn't *want* to believe it would actually happen?

6

Sesame

NIGHT PASSES. Somehow I sleep, on and off, feeling guilty every time I wake up. Like, how can I sleep when Micah's been taken? Is *he* sleeping, wherever he is? I try to beam him my thoughts: *We're looking for you, Micah. We will find you.* In my mind I tell him about the flyers I'm going to put up before tutoring, about the missing person report, about Inky and Sebastian. I don't tell him that Officer Emmanuel isn't worried, and I don't tell him how expensive the flyers were even with the 50 percent discount, and I don't tell him how worried I am. None of that would be fair to him.

I hope he's safe.

I hope he's sleeping.

If he's not sleeping, I hope he can feel me thinking about him.

My house is freezing when I wake up for the last time at five a.m. The electric fireplace is cranked as high as it can go, but this is the kind of deep freeze that penetrates everywhere. I pull on all my layers, and out into the dark we go, the flyers and me and the staple gun that my former neighbors Brian and Chee gave me when they moved to China. Thank you, Brian and Chee, for also giving me three full boxes of staples. Thank you, kind FedEx Office clerk, for giving me that discount. Thank you, telephone poles, for being so solid and strong. Thank you, staples, for being tough enough to drive into these telephone poles. Thank you, fingers, for being tough enough to keep centering the flyers on the poles and pulling the staple gun trigger even though you are so cold I can't feel you. Thank you, Inky and Sebastian, for being my friends and spreading the word about Micah.

Sometimes it helps to say thank you. Just say it over and over. No matter what is happening, say thank you.

I manage to staple up fifty flyers, here and there around Uptown, before I have to hustle to Greenway Elementary and meet Vong. Vong is many things—tiny and serious and strange and funny—but late is not one of them. Vong has been my tutoree for a year now. Our goal is clear: help him attain grade level in reading and writing. Tutoring Vong is both an official internship through my school, New World

Online Academy, and a part-time paid job. Which I need, because life? Is expensive.

Vong is waiting for me in the reading room when I rush in. I'm only three minutes late, but he's tapping the big watch on his wrist. What kind of second grader wears a big analog watch on his wrist? Answer: Vong's kind of second grader.

"Why are you so mad?"

That's the first thing he says. Like I said, there is nothing light about this kid. Even when he insists on talking with his fake British accent, he's deadly serious about it.

"I'm not mad."

"You're *something* then."

"I'm fine. A little worried is all."

"About what?"

"Jeez, kid. What are you, my personal therapist?"

He says nothing. He doesn't blink. From experience, I know that he won't say anything either, or turn to the writing we're supposed to be doing, until I've answered to his satisfaction.

"I'm worried about Micah. He's gone missing."

His eyes widen. He loves Micah, who sometimes walks with me to Greenway Elementary or waits for me in the office until Vong and I are done for the day.

"Then we have to find him."

"I'm working on it."

"I want to help."

This gets me. Vong's seven years old. He's tiny. I mean,

he literally has to put rubber bands around that giant watch of his in order to keep it from sliding up and down his arm. How can he possibly help? But, okay. Inspiration strikes me.

"Tell you what, why don't you write a poem for him?"

It took me a long time to figure out something—anything—that would get Vong writing. It was only after we went to the school library and I spotted *The Gashlycrumb Tinies* by Edward Gorey that the magic door opened. He loves that book. Which is really creepy when you think about it. I mean, every Tiny is a kid who dies in a different random way, like being thrown out of a sleigh or smothered under a rug, but it's also one of the funniest books I've ever read.

Vong nods decisively. He's all business when it comes to poems. He gets to work with his colored pencils and his eraser and his poems notebook, and by the end of the hour, (a) he's worked on his writing and penmanship and syntax and rhyme, (b) I've helped him with all of the above, and (c) he's written a finished poem. Missions accomplished, all of them. He rips the poem out of the notebook and hands it to me.

> Roses are red,
> violets are blue.
> Sesame and I
> will find you.

"Give it to Micah, okay?"
"Vong, I don't know where he is."

"When you *find* him," he says, with a major eye roll.

Okay then. Thank you, Vong, for helping the hour pass.

I spend the morning and early afternoon, before it's time to walk Prince and Peabop, putting the flyers into my poem boxes and stapling them onto poles. By three p.m., half are gone. It's clear I'm going to have to make a lot more. Until we find him, the flyers will be an ongoing expense, and I don't know how I'm going to pay for them, but I push that to the back of my mind. I think about texting the Jameses to tell them what's going on with Micah. I should talk to them before Officer Emmanuel does, right? But that conversation feels like too much to handle right now, so I push that to the back of my mind too. Later. Maybe tonight.

On the way to the Jameses' house, I organize my thoughts for the search. Police report filed, missing person flyers posted, social media report to come later from Inky and Sebastian. If they'd heard anything, they would've texted me.

What to look for:

1. Abandoned buildings.
2. An old white passenger van with a GOT HOCKEY? bumper sticker, which according to Micah is the Prophetmobile.
3. ??? Is this really all I have to go on—an abandoned building and a white passenger van?

I force myself not to panic by recalling everything I've learned about cults. How sometimes cult members hide away in remote places, like the mountains of Idaho or in underground caverns in the desert, but how sometimes cults exist side by side with ordinary people, in big cities or small towns.

"Don't call them a cult," Micah said the first time I used the term. This was a year ago.

"Aren't they, though?"

"Not according to them."

"What about according to you?"

He was silent. He was burning on the inside. I could feel it. We knew what each other was thinking. We *know* what each other *is* thinking. Don't use the past tense, Sesame. Micah's not dead. He's just disappeared. He's somewhere close by. He has to be.

He wouldn't have gone with them if his parents hadn't been part of it. His parents had been worn down, down, down by the Prophet until the tipping point was reached and they metaphorically tipped back into the arms of the Living Lights like they were playing a game of metaphorical Trust. They let their minds go soft and limp, and they trusted the Living Lights to catch them.

And the Lights caught them. Boy did they.

You wouldn't catch me playing Trust, not even when I was little. Why would I? Why would anyone? What if they let you fall? Then where would you be? Crumpled on the ground, is where, instead of straight and tall with all your bones unbroken. My grandmother taught me to hold back, to keep things to myself. She believed in self-protection. "Protect yourself, my girl," she used to say.

When it was clear that the Living Lights had sunk their talons but good into Micah's parents—when they were at the point that anything he said about the Prophet or the Living Lights Project was going straight over their heads—Micah decided that if worse came to worst, he would go with them. Because he was worried, right? Which I get. But.

"It's not a good idea," I said. "You have to protect yourself."

"I have to protect them, too, though," he said. "Think of it this way: I'll be kind of like an embedded reporter."

"Embedded reporters go to war, Micah."

"Embedded reporters are the conscience of the world, Ses."

"Embedded reporters sometimes get killed. Have you thought of that?"

"They're my *parents*," he said, and the way he said it made me see how worried he was about them. "If it was your grandmother, wouldn't you want to be with her?"

I just shook my head. My grandmother was dead and she had been dead for two years already at that point.

"Micah," I said, "listen to me. Do not underestimate the power of charisma."

He just laughed.

"Charisma? The Prophet? Please."

Most people think of charisma as a good thing. A charm

thing, a magnetic personality thing, a leader-of-people thing. Not me. Charisma can be all those things, but charisma can also be a cover for bottomless greed. Greed for power. Control. Attention. Fame. People tend not to think about charisma in those terms, but they should. I mean, Hitler had charisma. Right?

This is only the second day, but it feels like forever. I keep waiting for a text or call from Inky or Sebastian, or from some unknown number that belongs to someone who saw one of my flyers and has information about Micah. But I just keep seeing those three phones in my mind. All lined up. Should I have taken your phone? No, that wouldn't make any difference. Wherever you are, you're not with your phone.

It's good that I have to walk Peabop and Prince. It's good to have to do something, right now, right away. Because, panic.

The dogs are waiting just behind the Jameses' front door, happy to see me. They're always happy to see me. Peabop is a border collie and Prince is a pit-poodle mix, which looks exactly as strange as you'd think. Prince always wears a purple bandanna because his owners, James One and James Two—yes, they both have the same name, and when they started dating, their friends began calling them James One and James Two—are Prince fans from back in the day. They used to go see him at First Avenue. There are photos of them standing next to his star on the wall there. They mourned for weeks when he died.

"What's your favorite Prince song?" they said when they interviewed me, and I thought fast.

"'Purple Rain,'" I said, which may or may not have been the only Prince song I knew at the time, and the name of which may or may not have arisen in my mind from the collective unconscious. Ever heard of Carl Jung and his theory of the collective unconscious? It says that our minds all contain memories and impulses that are common to all humanity, and that we are born with them already in our brain. Like if you live in Minneapolis, you're born with knowledge of Prince.

The Jameses both closed their eyes and pursed their lips and nodded when I said "Purple Rain." The thing is, though, I *am* a Prince fan now. James One and James Two were right: he's great. Sometimes when the dogs and I walk around Bde Maka Ska, I put on my earbuds and my Prince playlist.

"Do you know, Sesame G.," James One said to me once—he always calls me Sesame G.—"Prince never abandoned his hometown. He never moved away from Minnesota."

My grandmother loved Minneapolis too, and she never moved away. Micah and I love Minneapolis, and our plan is to open a café here. James One and James Two have already said they want to be our first customers. They're crazy about Micah's cooking. They're crazy about Micah, too.

"Sesame, please tell me this fine young man is your

sweetheart," James One said the first time they met Micah, after he'd walked the dogs with me and we brought them back to their house.

"Yes, please tell us that you two are an item," James Two said. "Because we heartily approve."

They had just met him! Like, three minutes before! And Micah was standing right there! But the Jameses could already tell what kind of person Micah is, and they were right. We all stood there, Micah with his arms around Peabop because she was cold, and I felt my whole head turn hot.

"James One, I believe we have embarrassed our girl," James Two said.

"We have indeed embarrassed her," James One said. "And all this time I was thinking she wasn't an embarrassable sort."

But I was. I am. Maybe embarrassed isn't the right word. Maybe the word is more like *When something is so important you can't talk about it, like how much this boy means to you, your whole body starts to burn*. Yeah. A word for that particular feeling would be the right word.

"Come on, sweet peas," I say now, and I clip the leashes to Peabop's and Prince's purple collars.

The Jameses are home when I bring Prince and Peabop back, which is weird. They're regular working people with regular jobs downtown. They're both in the kitchen, back door unlocked, waiting for me. Oh crap, maybe Officer

Emmanuel already called them. Peabop and Prince seem surprised to see them too.

"What's going on?" I say. "Are you guys okay?"

My voice sounds weird even to me. James One looks at me closely. "We sense a disturbance in the Force."

James Two is looking at me now too, with the same look of concern on his face. "The question is are *you* okay, Sesame?" he says.

"Yeah."

"You sure?" James One says.

They are standing by the sink in their kitchen. Peabop and Prince are gulping from their water bowls so fast the water splashes onto the splash mats beneath. It's like they haven't had anything to drink in days. They're water-holic dogs.

"Yeah. I'm sure."

James Two puts his hand up in the air between him and me and turns to James One and starts talking as if I can't hear him. Like his hand in the air makes some kind of sound barrier between them and me. James Two: "Ask her about him." James One: "But what if her heart's broken?" James Two: "Then it's even more important we ask her." Then they both nod at each other and turn back to me. James Two drops his hand back by his side and clears his throat.

"Sesame," he says. "Here's the deal. We got a call from an Officer Emmanuel. She said that you listed us as emergency contacts? And that your aunt is out of town? And you're concerned about Micah?"

I'm afraid to look up. Afraid of what they'll say. What else did Officer Emmanuel tell them? The Jameses aren't my family, after all. I don't have any family. Not that anyone but Micah knows that.

"Oh!" I say. "I'm so sorry. I should've told you. I put you down because my aunt is in California with her friend, she's really sick, my aunt's taking care of her, she won't be back for like a month and the officer wanted to check in with, you know, my people—" I stop because "my people" hurts to say. Makes my throat close up a little. Who are my people? My grandma was my people. Micah is my people. Sebastian and Inky are my people. And the Jameses. Unless they aren't, and my giving out their names and phone numbers was overstepping. I'm afraid to look at them again.

"Sesame," James Two says. "It's okay."

"Yeah," James One says. "It's okay, honey."

The honey undoes me. Tears start leaking out again. The Jameses both put an arm around me. Peabop and Prince stand in front of us, tails wagging.

"It's fine for you to put us down as contacts," James Two says. "In fact, we were flattered."

"Yeah," James One says. "That's not what we're concerned about. Our question is, what's going on with Micah?"

I swallow. There's a lump in my throat. This is what the Jameses do to me. This is what kindness does to me. James One and James Two are looking at me closely, both of them nodding.

"You can tell us," James Two encourages me. The lump in my throat swells and hurts and the tears keep coming and the Jameses are leading me over to the couch—big and white, with blankets spread over it so Peabop's and Prince's claws don't scratch the leather—and sitting me down between them.

"Spit it out now," says James One, and James Two takes my hand between his.

So I do. I tell them everything, that Micah and his parents have disappeared, that the Living Lights have swallowed them up, it's already been two days, I don't know where he is, they left their phones behind. I tell the Jameses that I filed a missing person report but Officer Emmanuel didn't seem worried and she hasn't called me and I put up a million missing person flyers and do they have any idea how expensive it is to make copies? And how all day long I've been waiting to hear Micah's text ringtone, which is crazy because again, he doesn't even have his phone!

"You think he's somewhere in the city?" James Two asks, after he and James One have sat there for a minute, absorbing everything.

"Yes."

"Why?"

"He left a message for us on the whiteboard in his kitchen. He said to look for his GPS somewhere in the neighborhood."

"But you don't have any specifics? He never mentioned

an address, or a place, or any identifying features?"

"The Prophet—that's what the leader calls himself— kept talking about this abandoned building he'd bought in South Minneapolis with all the money they gave him. He calls it the South Compound. I think that's where they are."

They glance at each other, and I can feel their hesitance. It sounds far-fetched, I know. But I'm sure Micah's somewhere nearby. I mean, there's the message on the whiteboard, and all the talk about the South Compound and how it was going to be the base of operations. And anyway, my gut says he's nearby, and the body knows things that the mind doesn't, right? We carry knowledge way down inside us. Like the Prophet. We both knew he was dangerous, like really dangerous, from the beginning. But we ignored it. We overrode our instincts. And now Micah is gone. I tell them all this.

They both nod, are quiet for a moment, thinking. Then James One says, "You want to stay with us while all this is going on? I mean until your aunt gets back?"

I swallow hard. They are so kind. I picture my house, dark and cold without me in it, my table of poems waiting to be scrolled up, my skylight and my quilts, and then I imagine myself here, with the Jameses. This house is theirs, and my house is mine. I can't give in. That would be weak. I take care of myself and I'm good at it. *Don't ask for help, Sesame. You want to change something, change it yourself.* And maybe the most important thing? My house is where Micah would go if he escapes. I shake my head.

"No," I say. "But thank you. Really, thank you."

"Anytime," James One says again. "We're worried too. What are you going to do right now?"

"Go make more flyers. I already stapled up most of the ones I made at FedEx Office last night."

"Hey!" James Two says, as if he has a great idea, and James One must have the same idea, because they both reach for their back pockets at the same time. "That's something we can do," James One says, and they each hand me some money. Twenties and tens. "Use this to make more flyers."

"Or, wait!" James Two says. "Let's make this even easier. Take the money and make more now, then give me a copy of the flyer and I'll make copies at work, as many as you need until he turns up. I'll leave them on the porch so you can swing by whenever you want and get them."

My throat hurts again. From crying and from them being so nice, I guess. I nod, take the money, zip up my jacket, and head out into the cold.

On the way to FedEx Office, I stop at Isles Bun & Coffee and get a cinnamon bun. Their cinnamon buns are the best bakery buns in the city, but Micah's are better. Everything Micah makes is better than anyone else's. Like his grilled cheese.

Micah's grilled cheese begins with butter and a hot pan.

He spreads soft butter on one side of the bread and places it butter-side down in the hot pan. He shaves off thin slices of cheddar with the knife he gave me, the one that sits on the butcher block with my spoons and forks, and layers them on the bread. He butters another slice of bread and places it butter-side up on top of the cheese. He covers the pan with a plate because I don't have a lid, and turns the flames down.

He waits. I wait with him. We stand at the burner. Little blue flames flicker beneath the pan, and the smell of melting butter and toasting bread is irresistible. After a minute, he takes the lid off and flips the grilled cheese with the spatula he gave me, so that the bottom can toast. The top is perfect: golden and crisp. He presses the spatula down on it and cheese oozes out the sides. He puts the lid back on and looks at me and smiles.

"Almost," he says. "Patience."

His patience is greater than mine. If it were me making that grilled cheese, it'd be half gone already, a paper towel wrapped around it to save using a plate. But not Micah. He waits until the bottom is as perfectly golden-crisp as the top.

Micah told me he spoke Food the first day we met, when I was making my poem rounds. I looked up and there he was, this boy, just looking at me. It took me a minute to recognize him. We had ridden the elementary school bus together, but I hadn't seen him since. He surprised me. Kind of scared me, too, that I hadn't noticed his footsteps. You have to be vigilant. You have to be on guard. You can't let people sneak up on you. Especially when you live the way I do. He was holding a Lunds bag in his arms.

"Hey," he said. "Sorry if I scared you."

I held the leashes—I was walking Prince and Peabop—out in front of me like a weapon.

"What's in the bag?" I said. It just popped out of my mouth.

Prince and Peabop sat back on their haunches and watched him quietly, this tall boy with dark curls and a Lunds grocery bag who somehow had materialized next to us. That neither Prince nor Peabop were afraid of him should've been a clue, but I was so angry at myself for letting my guard down that I didn't even notice they weren't barking and lunging.

Looking back, that I myself didn't notice Micah's sudden appearance in the alley should've been another clue. That he was friend, not foe. That my gut knew something my conscious mind didn't, which was that I could trust him.

"Potatoes," he said.

My right hand clutched the leash and my left hand was folded around a couple of scrolled-up poems that I was about to drop into the poem box hidden behind me. I just stared at him. I was determined not to give anything away. But . . . potatoes? For real? Potatoes are so, like, old-school.

"I like potatoes," I said. That didn't seem like enough, though. Like if Vong wrote down *I like potatoes*, I would tell him to be more specific, add detail, give the reader a glimpse of personality. So I kept going. "Mashed are my favorite."

He smiled. "Mashed are good. Baked are good. So are fried. It's hard to ruin a potato."

Then he said, "I know you, don't I?" and it was the way he said it that made me look hard at him. Not like, *I know you because I think you go to my high school,* or *I know you because we used to ride the same school bus in elementary school,* but in a bigger way. Like he knew before I did why I wasn't afraid of him, why I was willing to talk about potatoes with him, why the topic of potatoes was the outside conversation but something else was happening below the words.

That can happen, you know. Sometimes you meet someone—you see them on the street or you turn your head in a restaurant or you bump into them on the light rail—and you know them. As if you've known them forever. As if in another world you knew them. We kept talking and I kept standing in front of the poem box so he wouldn't see it. Peabop and Prince eventually got bored and lay down, right in the snow, in a patch of sunlight a leash's length away.

I was thinking about that day as I walked to FedEx Office. My hand holding the white waxed-paper bag with the Isles cinnamon bun was frozen. The other one was tucked down into my pocket, which was how I knew my phone was ringing even though I could only feel the vibration. I hauled it out and sank down on the sidewalk.

Unknown number. My heart flooded with hope. *Please be Micah*, I thought, *please be Micah*, as I swiped it open.

"Miss Gray?"

Shit.

"Officer Emmanuel?"

"Yes. Sesame, I'm calling with an update. I spoke with one of the Southwest High School vice principals this afternoon, and she informed me that Micah has an excused absence until winter break starts after school next Friday."

"What?"

"His parents sent in an excuse note two weeks ago, well in accordance with the ten-day minimum requirement. Apparently, Micah and his parents are headed south on an extended camping trip through winter break."

"That's not true," I say. My voice is barely audible. I clear my throat. "That's not true!"

Officer Emmanuel is silent for a minute. "What makes you think so, Sesame?"

"Because it's not true!" I cry. "They've been *stolen*! They're all hiding in the South Compound!"

Again I sound like I'm the one who can't be believed. I explain to her that the Stones aren't the camping type, that they sold their car, that they don't have any money because the Prophet took it all, that they've been brainwashed, that someone made them write that note, that Micah would *never* miss seven days of school because he's a good student and he loves school and he's not like me, who wouldn't care if she never set foot in school again and on and on and on, and Officer Emmanuel listens to me for a while, but then she interrupts.

"Sesame," she says. "Please, Sesame. Try to calm down. There was nothing unusual about the excuse note, and given the lack of any other red flags with the Stones, either parents or son, I'm sorry, but it appears that everything is in order."

I don't answer. What can I say that I haven't already said? In a horrible way, I can even understand why she's not going to do anything. They've covered all their bases. Micah's excused from school until after winter break. I do some quick mental arithmetic. As of today, it will be twenty-four days before school starts again and Micah doesn't show up.

"Please update us if you find out anything else, though," Officer Emmanuel says when I don't say anything. "Thank you, Sesame. Keep the faith."

I barely hear her. So much can happen in twenty-four days. In the hands of someone like the Prophet, twenty-four days is enough to break someone.

7

Micah

DEAR WORLD,

I'm writing this missive in my head while sitting on my army cot here in the Room of Micah closet. I would write it for real, in coded notes in the Hello Kitty notebook using the Hello Kitty pencil, but I've stopped doing that. If someone finds them, I'd lose more infraction points. I'm already down to seventy-five.

Prophet (holding up one of the white robes I washed and hung up to dry in the laundry room): "You call this white, Stone?"

Me: "Well, I'd call it white-*ish*, Prophet. What about you?"

Prophet: "I call it filthy. Filthy thoughts beget filthy

robes beget infractions. Minus five points, Stone."

Me: "But wouldn't the mind that sees filth be a filthy mind, Prophet?"

Prophet: "Transgression. Minus another five."

Me (starting to say something, but interrupted by a small-voiced Sandra Stone): . . .

Sandra: "Please, Prophet. He didn't mean it."

Prophet: "He did mean it, Sandra. But that is why we are here in the South Compound. We are gathered together to retrain our minds and hearts in the ways of Living Lights, that we may abandon the secular world and go forth in the full knowledge of the kingdom that awaits those who adhere to the principles and blah blah blah blah blah blah blah blah . . ."

Oh, sorry, Prophet. I lost track there. Which is probably why, you guessed it, he minused me another five infraction points.

Did my mom protest? No. She bowed her head and put her hands together, like everyone else after the Prophet speaks. Did my dad protest when I talked to them about it later in the dining room? Not really. I mean, he frowned and shook his head, but then he said, "You've got to be careful, Micah."

"Of what?" I said.

"Of your thoughts. Of your actions. That's why we're here."

"Is it, Dad? Could you tell me why again, exactly, it is that we're here?"

"To examine the way we're living our lives, Micah. To take stock. To make sure we're on the right path."

I looked down at my plate. White bread, white mayonnaise, white cheese, raw cauliflower, tapioca pudding. Why is everything white? Robes, food, walls: white. No one questions it, though. If I question it, I'll probably get more infraction points. It's been, what, three days? Four? I'm losing track.

"Am I not on the right path, Dad? Is that why I'm the only one with an infractions point chart? Is that why I'm the only one living in a closet? Oh, excuse me, I mean 'Room of Micah.'"

My mother cleared her throat. "What Dad is saying, Micah, is that nothing is easy here in the compound, and nothing is *meant* to be easy. The harder things are, the more we are tested. The more we are tested, the truer the mettle of our character will be forged."

What does that even mean? She's talking the way the Prophet talks. They're all starting to. Even the little kids, who are all the kids except for me. There are grown-ups, and there are little kids, and then there's me. No-man's-land Micah. Neither here nor there Micah. No one knows what to do with Micah, except the Prophet and his sidekick Deeson seem to have a plan. It's like they can see right through me to my jeering mind, like they anticipated my rebellion and planned for it.

"One more infraction, Stone, and you will be placed on permanent duty in the laundry room," the Prophet said.

"You will sleep there, you will eat there, you will wash and wash and wash again until the robes of the Living Lights congregants are sufficiently white."

I managed not to say anything, even though his eyes were daring me to. My parents stood by anxiously—I guess they were waiting for my next infraction too—but I stayed silent, and the Prophet walked away.

The weird thing? That the little kids down here seem to enjoy it. It's like they're on extended playground time even though they have chores and Reflection and Living Light training just like everyone else. But they make a game of everything, like who can eat the slowest, or who can go the longest without saying anything, or who can sing the loudest when it comes to Songs of Praise. From behind my closed closet door, I hear them whispering in their Rooms of Sleeping until way after they're supposed to be asleep. Jerald and Krystyna have emerged as the de facto leaders of each room. Their voices travel under the closed doors of the Rooms of Sleeping and down the hall, then under my closed closet door. So does their laughter. Everyone loves Jerald and Krystyna, even the Prophet and Deeson. They even smile when they see them traipsing along the hall in their miniature white robes.

Maybe they see themselves in Jerald and Krystyna, as leaders, as the ones the others look up to. Dream on, Prophet and Deeson. No one looks up to either of you. They might think they do—I've seen the way Andrea K. and Gregory M. glance at each other and nod when one of you starts in with a new lecture—but the truth? They're afraid of you.

They're right to be afraid of you, but fear will keep them down. Fear will keep them doing exactly what you tell them to do, which is rise, eat, wash, reflect, chores, study, sing, eat, wash, reflect, chores, study, eat, wash, reflect, sleep. Same schedule for everyone.

My Life as a Fake Member of a Doomsday Cult.

Pretend Cultist.

The Cult of the Living Lights.

I hate my chore. I hate the laundry room. I hate its damp cold. I hate the two big steel tubs here in the laundry room: one for wash, one for rinse. Cold water only. A washboard like you see in antiques stores. Dump the clothes in the cold water, scrub them up and down the washboard. Dump them in the rinse water. Rinse once. Rinse twice. Rinse thrice. Wring them out with your hands, which, do you have any idea how hard that is? Hang them up on the lines that weave back and forth above my head. Then try to avoid the *drip drip drip* of gravity pulling the water out of the wet clothes down onto the cement floor. Pretend you're writing instead of wringing out cold heavy cotton.

Doing laundry is hell on your hands. How did washerwomen hundreds of years ago do it? My hands are cracked. They bleed. It happens faster than you'd think, especially in winter in a basement compound heated with, count them, three space heaters. You know what I've started doing when we eat? Spreading mayonnaise on the white bread and then scraping some off and rubbing it on my hands underneath the table. There's no lotion, no oil, nothing else to keep the skin of my hands from breaking open.

It's rough. All the food is white, all the walls are white, and all the clothes are white, which is the reason for the bleach on top of the detergent. White robes. White underwear. Yeah, that's right. I get to wash everyone's underwear. I can't stand this laundry room another minute right now, so I sneak down the hall to the Room of Secular Refuse. The Room of Secular Refuse has a couch, which I'm sitting on, and a table. The Prophet and Deeson use the table to display items of secular refuse, like an unopened condom and a bank debit card.

"There is no use for these items in the South Compound," the Prophet said at lunch. He held the condom and the debit card up in front of the whole dining room, as if they were filthy. "All items such as these will be confiscated and placed in the Room of Secular Refuse."

I sat there with my parents, not looking at them nor they at me. Did they think the condom was mine? Because it's not. Neither is the bank debit card. I snuck a look at it when I slipped in here after finishing the laundry: *Andrea K.* What was she thinking? She and all the other adults were supposed to pool their money, like, all their money, and give it to the Prophet to use for the Living Lights Project.

I distract myself by thinking about Sesame and our plans. We're going to build our own raft and float down

Minnehaha Creek this summer, as close to the falls as we can get. We're going to learn how to spin fire. We're going to build an ice sculpture for the luminaria on Lake of the Isles in February. We're going to open a café in Minneapolis when we're through high school, after we couch-surf around the world. It's going to be a combination poetry café and art gallery, a place where people can come for delicious food and beautiful poems and art that they won't be able to stop looking at. We won't have any menu categories like breakfast and lunch and dinner because why? If something is delicious, does it matter what time of day you eat it?

We're working on a good name for the café. Sesame wants it to be a line from one of her favorite poems, like Let Ruin End Here or I Contain Multitudes, but I want a food name, like Grape or Onion or Mango or Potato. A simple name of a simple food that has been around forever, a food that makes you feel warm and happy when you hear it. I wouldn't say we argue about the name, but we definitely haven't come to an agreement yet.

We agree on the menu, though. It'll be small because huge menus are exhausting. As long as every option is delicious, it's better to have only a few options. Our goal is when you taste the food in our café, you'll want to close your eyes because it tastes so good, the way my mom closes her eyes when I put a plate of spinach lasagna in front of her. You'll want to move into the café and live there so you can eat every meal there. It won't be just the food, either, it'll be the way the place feels. Like home, like you're known and loved the minute you walk in the door. The way home should be, anyway.

Home. That wouldn't be such a bad name.

Our café won't be expensive. Plus, one day a week will be donation-based, where you pay what you want. There'll be a basket of scrolled-up poems by the cash register so you can take one on your way out. If you'd like to paint a piece of art for us, please do, and if it's beautiful, we'll hang it on the wall. Our definition of beautiful is broad, so don't worry.

See? This is how I distract myself. I think of anything but the basement laundry room and my bleeding hands.

Do you feel any different now, Micah, now that you're underground?

No.

Really? You're a member of a cult that's fled to a basement compound, though, aren't you?

I'm not a member of the cult.

You sure about that?

Yes.

You don't feel yourself slipping even a tiny bit? All that white food? All those white robes? All that bleached underwear? I mean, it's weird not seeing the outside world, isn't it? What if no one's noticed you're gone? What if everyone believes the note your parents sent to school and thinks you're on an extended camping trip with them?

They won't. Sesame won't, anyway.

You sure?

Yes. I'm sure—99 percent sure, anyway.

Then: *Knock. Knock.* Which jolts me out of my thoughts, because these knocks are real. Someone's at the door of the Room of Secular Refuse, which is where I'm hiding before dinner.

Knock. Knock.

My heart races. Who is it? Do they know I'm in here? Did I transgress again? I didn't, did I? I finished the laundry, I used plenty of bleach, I made sure the Prophet's robe is especially white, I rinsed out the tubs, I made prayer hands at Deeson when I passed him in the hall, I didn't complain about the sandwiches of whiteness at lunch. In fact, I didn't say anything. I haven't said anything all day.

Knock. Knock.

"Come in!" I yell. Is that the right thing to say? Should I have jumped up and opened the door? It's not locked, is it? Did I lock it? Is it against the rules to lock a door?

KNOCK. KNOCK.

Maybe they didn't hear me yell, "Come in!" In desperation, I jump up and open the door, which wasn't locked. Deeson is on the other side. Deeson with his eyes that are looking deader and deader, like the Prophet's eyes. Dead-Eye Deeson.

"Transgression," he says. "Minus five points."

"Yeah? What was my infraction?"

"Insubordination. Not being where you are supposed to be."

"Which is where? I finished the laundry and it's not dinnertime yet."

"Read the schedule. Reflection. Everyone else is there, including your parents."

"Can I ask you a question, Deeson? Mr. Deeson, I mean? I mean Acolyte Deeson?"

His dead eyes just look at me. But he doesn't say no, so I risk it.

"Does that condom on the table belong to you, Acolyte Deeson? It's not my brand, so . . . I was just wondering."

Deeson's dead eyes flare to life, if hatred is a form of life.

"Insubordination!" he thunders.

I chime in with him on the next line: *"Infraction!"*

And just like that, I'm down to sixty-five points.

8

Sesame

THE LIBRARIAN AT the checkout desk looks up at me
when I pass the counter and smiles. She's known me since I
was little. My grandmother and I used to live in this library,
and I mean that semi-literally. We were here for story hour,
movie nights, holiday crafts, lectures, you name it. I smile
back at her, a real smile, and then I push open the door to
the conference room. Inky and Sebastian are already there.

Inky's doing that thing with her hair where she twirls a
curl around and around and then lets it spring. Sebastian,
who's freakishly double-jointed, is folding one finger
over the other over the other, on and on until his hands
are clumped-up balls of twisted fingers. Both are habits

done only when they're anxious or upset. My stomach clenches.

"So, Ses," Sebastian begins, and I hold up my hand.

"Sebastian, if you're about to tell me that everything's fine and that they're on a camping trip, don't."

Sebastian closes his mouth. Inky twirls another curl.

"That excuse note is a lie," I say. Neither one looks at me, so I say it again, enunciating each word. "A *lie*. They're covering their tracks. As instructed by the Prophet."

Sproing goes the curl. Sebastian untwists one of his claw hands. He clears his throat.

"How exactly do you know that?" he asks.

"Because Micah would have told me. Did Officer Emmanuel call you?"

He shrugs. I turn to Inky, who's got both hands imprisoned in her curls now, one on either side of her head. "She called you, too?"

Inky doesn't say anything. Instead, she sproings her fingers free, reaches down into her backpack, and hauls up a lidded cup of coffee. *Sester* is scrawled on it. Her name for me, a combo meal of Sister and Sesame. Stupid but not, because she thought it up when we were in second grade together at Lake Harriet Elementary, and that's a pretty smart nickname for a seven-year-old. She pushes it across to me and I cradle it in my hands beneath the table in case anyone official walks by the glass wall and sees me with it. No one ever has, but still. *No beverages or food*. I slip the lid off and hold it up to my nose before I take the first sip. Cappuccino. Cinnamon sprinkled across the foam. Inky knows the exact way I love my coffee: dark and strong and cinnamony.

"You guys," I say, "here's the thing. I get that no one official is going to do anything, at least not yet, because of the note and the lack of any reported neglect. But *you* get that we don't have that kind of time, right?"

Last night, when I couldn't sleep, I'd googled *how long does it take to die of hypothermia/dehydration/starvation*.

"I mean, we don't know where he is, and we don't know what conditions he's living under," I continue. "A person can die of dehydration in as little as a few days. Of hypothermia in less than a day. Of starvation in less than three weeks."

"Okay, Ses," Inky says. "It's just—" I put my hand up to stop her the same way I stopped Sebastian.

"It's just nothing," I say. "Are you with me here?"

I can still see doubt on their faces. In my head I beg them: *Please. Please be with me.* They must sense it, because they look at each other, then at me, and they nod. Real nods.

"Yes," Sebastian says.

I wait a beat, to make sure. Inky nods.

"We've gotten a bunch of messages," Sebastian says, changing the subject. "Mostly just the 'oh that's awful I hope you find him' kind. A few possible sightings, but none that sound remotely like Micah."

"It's like people see something online and then they

just randomly call or text with a tip that makes no sense," Inky says. "Like, oh, this'll be helpful!"

"Not," Sebastian says. "What else can we do at this point?"

"We need to look for him," I say.

"But—where?" Inky says, after a pause. "How?"

I feel panicky. South Minneapolis is a big place.

"We just . . . search," I say. "Walk every block of South Minneapolis. Check out every abandoned building we find. And every single white passenger van, because Micah says that's what the Prophet drives. He says the van has a 'Got Hockey?' bumper sticker on it, but if you see a van that doesn't, check it out anyway. Bumper stickers can be removed."

"You're serious?" Inky says. "Wander around looking for abandoned buildings?"

"Yep. And white passenger vans."

They exchange glances, as if my plan doesn't make any sense. And maybe it doesn't, to them. But I know a lot more about abandoned buildings than they do. Even if an abandoned building looks dark and empty and unlived-in, someone might be living in it anyway.

"It's dark out already," Sebastian points out.

"She means tomorrow, dumb-ass," Inky says, and turns to me for confirmation.

"Daylight hours," I say. "That's what I'll be doing every daylight hour when I'm not tutoring or walking the pups: searching for him."

"What about school?"

"I only have one paper due before winter break. Big deal. I'll write it at night. Micah's out there somewhere."

Inky and Sebastian sit in silence for a minute; then Inky looks up at me.

"This is so scary," she says. "I guess I don't really want to think it can possibly be real. But if it is—"

"Then we have to do everything we can," Sebastian says. "Beginning now."

The thing is, though, Inky and Sebastian both have extra work shifts right now—pre-Christmas craziness. But they're covering social media, and that's big. Plus, I can cover a lot of ground myself during the daylight hours. I'll be the literal boots on the ground and they'll be the virtual boots. We all stand up and head out, Inky to Spyhouse, Sebastian to Kowalski's, me to . . . where? I don't want to go home.

It's been more than two years since my grandmother died. But even after all this time, sometimes, when I'm tired or so stressed I can't think straight, it's the little apartment above Soren the cobbler on Lyndale that I start walking to. When I think of *home*, that's what I think of.

My grandma was actually my mother, but she was so much older when she adopted me that everyone assumed she was my grandmother. We got tired of correcting people early on, so we just let it stand. The Safe Haven law in Minnesota says that if a mother decides not to keep her newborn baby, she can leave it with a hospital employee at a licensed hospital, no questions asked. That's what happened with me. My birth mother, whoever she was, gave me to the ER receptionist at Abbott Northwestern Hospital, and they gave me to my grandmother. She was originally my foster mother. Except that she failed at being a foster mother, because she ended up adopting me.

"I loved you at first sight," she said. "The way you followed me around with those dark eyes. Like you knew I was yours."

When I came home from school she was always in the apartment, listening to talk radio or Dolly Parton and chopping things for dinner. I would do my homework at the kitchen table while she cooked. My grandmother was a cafeteria lady at an elementary school in Saint Paul, and sometimes she told me stories about the little kids in the lunchroom. Like the girl who ate her apple from top to bottom instead of around. Like the boy who wore a different-color bow tie every day.

My grandma liked to do my hair, and I liked the feeling of her hands on my head. Braids and buns and complicated curving ponytails. In the beginning, after she died, I buzz-cut it with clippers. Simple. Quick. That way I didn't have to miss the way she did my hair. I didn't have to think about the things she used to tell me while I sat there and she stood behind me. The problem is, I think about them anyway.

My grandmother didn't believe in asking for help, and she didn't have many friends. Or maybe *any* friends.

Acquaintances, for sure. But friends? She never had anyone over to the apartment—she was a naturally wary person— and neither did I. It wasn't something I thought about. I just absorbed it from her, I guess.

But my grandmother also liked to laugh.

"Crimp the hell out of them," she used to say when we made pot stickers, which we did every Sunday. It made me laugh, the way she'd bend her fingers like claws and press them into the dough. Now, though, I look back on it differently. When she said, "Crimp the hell out of them," did she mean that for more than dumplings? My grandma was a small, quiet cafeteria lady at an elementary school, raising a girl young enough to be her granddaughter, and at the very end of her life, when she looked at me, did she want me to live a different kind of life? Because her last words were not *change it yourself* or *be vigilant* or *protect yourself*. Her last words were these:

"Don't be afraid like me, Sesame."

She said that right before she died. I didn't have a chance to ask her what she meant, but I've thought about it ever since. That one sentence has kind of rearranged my memories of my grandmother and added a layer onto them. When she sat up late playing solitaire and listening to the radio, was she afraid? Was she lonely?

"I have you," she used to say. "And that's enough for me."

I never questioned that when I was a kid, but I question it now. When she died, I fell into a hole. There was no one to take her place, to be a stand-in grandmother. We had lived a walled-off life in our apartment, just the two of us. Me and her at the kitchen table, doing homework, chopping vegetables, crimping pot stickers together.

Don't be afraid like me, Sesame.

It rings in my head now. I haven't ever told Micah about it. I haven't told anyone. I can barely think about it myself. It hurts too much to think that my grandma might have lived an afraid life all those years. That when she used to tell me that all she needed was me, maybe she wasn't telling the truth? My grandmother taught me a lot, but she didn't teach me how to be with other people. How to reach out to them. How to ask for help. Asking for help isn't in my nature, not even with Sebastian and Inky. I mean, they don't even know where I live. Or that I live alone.

Is that weird?

Yes, it's weird, I answer myself.

But I don't know how to fix it.

On the way home from the library, I walk past the Jameses' house. Their lamps are lit and their curtains are drawn, but I picture them inside with Prince and Peabop, and the image makes me feel warm. The Jameses live in a big house a couple of blocks from Lake Bde Maka Ska, not far from me. Each of the Minneapolis lakes, which thread their way through South Minneapolis, has its own look and its own personality. Lake of the Isles is the curvy lake, inlets and outlets and trees and islands. It's also the rich people's lake.

The houses are huge—they're mansions, most of them—and their lawns are wide and gracious, with canopied trees and wrought-iron handrails on the curving steps. It's a beautiful lake, but it's not Micah's and my lake. Lake Harriet is the charming family lake in the charming family neighborhood of Linden Hills. Little kids run around on its sand beaches, there's a performing stage that looks like a castle, there's a restaurant and racks of kayaks and canoes for rent. It's a sweet lake, but it's not our lake.

Our lake is Bde Maka Ska, which is the Dakota name for "White Earth Lake." Bde Maka Ska is three miles around, like most of the city lakes. Like almost all of them, there are walking paths and biking paths, beaches and picnic areas, playgrounds. I think of Bde Maka Ska as the international lake. It's our game to count up all the different languages we hear around it when I'm out walking Prince and Peabop and Micah's keeping me company. Somali and Hmong and Chinese and Russian and Spanish are the languages we recognize, but there are other ones that are unfamiliar to me. We don't know any languages ourselves besides English.

Sometimes we slow down or pick up the pace so that we can lag just behind a group of people speaking an unfamiliar language. If we absorb enough of it, maybe all our language skills will get better. That's my theory. I'm basing it off Jung's theory of the collective unconscious.

Micah was the one who taught me about Jung. He keeps a file of Jung quotes in a text thread to himself. He's memorized some of them. His favorite, which he paraphrased because (a) he thought it sounded clunky and (b) it was translated from German: *The darkness that we do not acknowledge in ourselves becomes the darkness we see in others.*

Micah, I hope it's not dark where you are.

A few months ago, the Prophet started telling Micah that cooking was one thing but that the idolatry of food was another and that he should forswear the preparation of food. That's when I knew that things had gone from creepy and wrong to dangerous. I mean, forbid someone to do what they most love to do? That's when all the sirens in the world should go off at once.

9

Micah

DEAR WORLD, this is how it began.

First the wine went.

Then the music.

Then the games.

Then the late nights.

Then the color. Literally, color. I came home from Sesame's house one night—I was gone for maybe five hours—and they were painting. Whitewashing. They were almost finished with the living room.

"What, are we living in an art gallery now?" I said. That's how flat and white the walls were, as if my parents were preparing for an installation. Except there would be no installation, because apparently, art was now added to the forbidden list. When you abandon the secular world, I guess you also abandon art. When I told Sesame the next day, I laughed. She didn't, though.

"They took down their paintings?" she said.

"Yeah."

"Did they take down the photos, too?"

Because our walls used to be covered with photos. Mostly of me as a baby, as a little kid, the three of us on family road trips. Lots of me standing on top of mountains holding my arms out to the sides, because that was my parents' thing. They liked to haul me to the top of a mountain, tell me to spread my arms as if I was about to jump, then take my photo.

"Of course. Photos are 'refuse from the secular world,' Ses. Exact quote."

I laughed again. But, again, she didn't. That's something else I think about now, me and Hello Kitty, down here in the South Compound. We both knew something was up, really up, but she didn't try to laugh it off the way I did.

"Micah," she said. "It's like this guy's read some kind of *How to Start a Cult* playbook. I mean, it's textbook."

She laid it out for me in a series of steps.

1. Anoint yourself as leader and call yourself a prophet.
2. Start talking with whoever will listen to you

about the Living Lights Project, and how it can help with the rigors of modern-day life. How it's a community that will take care of everything for you.

3. Come up with a plan that will require both subservience and money on the part of the ones who start following you.

4. Give your followers uniforms. Create rituals particular to the community. Start using language particular only to the community.

It's weird, but until she laid it out like that, I hadn't thought of the cult as a real cult, with an actual mastermind leader and an actual thought-out plan. I hadn't even noticed the random capitals in the daily e-mails—I had just gotten used to them, like everything else that came from the Prophet. The last few months aboveground, my parents started printing out e-mails from the Prophet, with all their random CaPitAls, as though they were too special to stay in the computer.

The days and nights are blending together now. I'm not sure how long we've been down here.

Right now, right at this minute, the world outside the compound is going on the way it always does. People are walking to school and work. They're getting on buses and behind the wheels of cars. Someone is looking up at the sky and shading their eyes from the sun. Or the snow. Or the wind. A father is telling his little kid to hurry up.

Another kid is telling her mother to slow down. People are eating food that isn't all white. Right? It's all still happening, isn't it? Sesame, what are you doing right this minute? Are you out there? Are you worried about me?

I'm not going to think of you right now.

Can't.

Hurts.

10

Sesame

AT GREENWAY Elementary on Monday morning, Vong sizes me up and frowns.

"You didn't find him yet?" he says.

I shake my head.

"Did you put my poem in a safe place?"

I nod. It's true. I put it in a green folder—green for Greenway Elementary—labeled *Vong*. It's on the poetry table in my house. He looks relieved. "My mom and me saw one of the Micah posters," he continues. "On Lyndale next to the Lotus restaurant. I told her who it was and she lit a candle for Micah when we got home."

My eyes fill up with tears when he tells me this. The

image of tiny Vong and his mother, who I've never met, lighting a candle for Micah. I brush away the tears, but Vong sees them anyway.

"We'll find him," he says. No trace of a British accent. No trace of anything except determination. "Don't worry, Miss Sesame."

Which is a crazy thing to say, because there's no way to stop worrying, but I nod anyway. We spend the rest of the hour working on pronouns and subjects, although I don't use those words with Vong. It's better to show, not tell. That's what my creative writing teacher at New World Online Academy says.

After I say goodbye to Vong, I immediately head out to begin searching. It's been five days and I'm in a routine: Make sure there are plenty of flyers in my backpack, along with water and an extra scarf if I need to wrap it around my face. Have a mental route map of at least six square blocks that covers both alley and street. Each six-square-block radius begins at a single poem box, which helps me, because of the poem thing.

The sky is gray and the snow flat white and everything looks downtrodden. I stand clutching my backpack, breathing in the cold air, wondering if I should start on the alley side or the street side today. Somehow it feels like a big decision, even though it isn't. Both sides will be covered. It's important to look at all sides of a building. Important to check for white passenger vans both front and back. I sounded so sure of myself in the conference room when I told Inky and Sebastian about abandoned buildings and white passenger vans, didn't I?

But in the light of day it's just . . . overwhelming. How do you start looking for someone who's trapped with a cult? Where do you even begin?

"Exactly the way you told Inky and Sebastian you would," I say out loud. "Just start walking. Don't be afraid."

Like me sounds in my head, in my grandmother's voice, but I don't say that out loud. I walk and search and post flyers simultaneously. Every daylight hour must be put to use. It's hard not to feel overwhelmed. It's hard not to feel panicked.

You know what's hardest, though? How lonely it is out here.

Which makes me think again of my grandma, and how she always said that I was enough, that she didn't need anyone but me. And I guess that sank into me from early on, because I just assumed I didn't need anyone but her. Then she died, and I found out it wasn't true.

Focus, Sesame.

I walk to today's poem box, at Grand and 31st, the epicenter of today's search. I open the box to restock it with flyers, and there's a note on a piece of notepaper there on top of the last of the flyers.

> *Roses are red*
> *violets are blue*
> *this poem is for you.*

I wish on the stars
I wish on the moon
that the boy who's gone
comes home soon.

The poem is written in kid handwriting, similar to Vong's but loopier. Whoever this kid poet is, they're thinking about Micah. And maybe they're also thinking about me, with the "this poem is for you" line. My eyes sting again. I look around, but no one's in the alley. I want Micah to see this new poem, and the poem that Vong wrote for him.

Someone in the house next to the poem box has strung little colored Christmas lights along their fence. Christmas is next week, and I haven't even thought about it. My grandmother and I didn't do much for Christmas, but we did put up a tree and she always gave me a gift she'd made. A hand-sewn stuffed bear one year, a knit stocking cap another year, a leather tool belt the next, one that she had cut and stitched together herself from some leftover leather that the cobbler, Soren, gave her. She cut it with an X-Acto knife, punched out holes with an awl, and threaded it with waxed thread. I didn't bring hardly anything with me from our old apartment, but I did bring that tool belt. And the bear. And the stocking cap is on my head this very minute.

I picture the green *Vong* folder on my poetry table at home. I look down at the "This poem is for you" poem in my hand.

And then I get an idea for a perfect Christmas gift for Micah. Every poem and every note that anyone writes for him or leaves in one of the poem boxes, I will collect and keep and give to him when we find him. That way, he'll know he wasn't forgotten. He'll know we were looking for him from the start. I picture him reading through the notes and poems. Micah in my house, reading and smiling: this is an image from a future I want to happen, and I hold on to it.

Beginning at the first poem box, I walk the alleys in my widening concentric squares. Alleys first today, instead of sidewalks. It's easier to spot an abandoned building from the alley: boarded-up windows, cracks in the foundation, rusted back entry doors leaning off their hinges—all these are more common on the alley side of a building. I go over every single scrap of information about the Prophet that Micah mentioned in past conversations.

Am I forgetting anything? The abandoned building in South Minneapolis. The white passenger van. The Living Lights Project. There's not a lot of specific detail, but it's important to remember everything I possibly can.

For so long, Micah thought the Prophet and the cult were funny—sad funny, cliché funny, old-Godzilla-movies funny. Then one day last summer he came to my house and told me his mom and dad had both quit their jobs, and he didn't laugh. He didn't text first, he just came over and knocked on the side door. Which is the only door, if you don't count the enormous one that rolls up in front, which

I don't. It would have startled me except that by then he had his own knock. Not a knock so much as a slide of his knuckles back and forth across the ridged metal surface. Like the wind, if the wind had hands, was the sound of Micah's knock. *Is* the sound of Micah's knock.

He just stood there when I opened the door. I had to reach out and pull him in before someone saw him. He knew better than to stand there—he knows that no one can know where I live—and that's how I knew it must be something bad.

"But how will they, like, buy groceries and pay the mortgage?" I asked when he told me they'd quit their jobs.

He shrugged, like that was the last thing that mattered. Which it wasn't. Isn't. It takes a lot of time and energy and scheming to earn your living. Trust me on that one.

"Maybe the Prophet's paying the bills or something?" he said at last.

Things got a lot clearer later on, when we found out about the "audit" part of the Living Lights plan. How the Prophet and Deeson went through all the congregants' finances and then told them how much each family was supposed to contribute. Which must have been a ton, right? I mean, if it was enough to buy the South Compound. A building in the middle of a big city, even if it's abandoned, costs a massive amount of money.

Micah wasn't clear on the whole audit thing, or how his parents would buy groceries. He was still being supported by his parents, like most people our age are. For example, my grandmother took care of all our bills. Even on her cafeteria-lady income, we always seemed to have enough money for food and rent. Once in a while, a trip to Target or dinner out at the Quang. How to afford things wasn't something she talked about. She took care of it.

It was only after she died that I learned all that stuff, and I learned it the hard way.

At the end, my grandmother might have felt she lived an afraid life, but she didn't show it. Although maybe she did? Maybe not having friends to the apartment, maybe always telling me to be vigilant and to protect myself and not to ask for help, or maybe not letting me have friends over was, in fact, showing she was afraid. This is the kind of thing I think about, now that she's gone.

Focus, Sesame.

Walk down the alley, looking left and right for signs of abandonment. Scan garages and parking lots for white vans, even regular vans, and examine them quickly but carefully look for signs of a GOT HOCKEY? bumper sticker or a recently removed bumper sticker. Take care to look ordinary, and not as if you're casing the neighborhood. Walk tall and straight and confident.

Even when things are ordinary, which they are the opposite of with Micah missing, routine keeps the days structured: Get up, dress, eat, tutor Vong, work on school assignments, walk the pups, meet up with Inky and Sebastian, see Micah, go to sleep. Rinse and repeat. That's my ordinary routine. I would give anything to be back in it.

As I walk, I think about the Stones, and the Living Lights Project, and the Prophet. Why didn't I do more to stop it, to convince Micah to stop it? I should've done more.

Because here's the thing: bad things start slow, and you ignore them because you think they'll go away. But they don't go away. They grow and grow until they've taken root, and once something sends down roots, it's hard to get rid of. It's like what Micah taught me about potatoes. All you need to make dozens of new potatoes is a single old potato that's grown an eye or two. You stick it eye-down in the ground and cover it with dirt and ignore it. Come back in a few months and dig. Prepare to be shocked.

You know what else started slow and took root? My grandmother's heart disease. By the time we knew what was happening, it was too late. And by the time Micah and I knew how far gone his parents were, it was too late. In both cases, the blind eye of the potato had sent down roots and grown too big to remove. By the time Micah tried to talk to them, they were in too deep.

"They won't listen to me," he told me, late another night when he just showed up at my door.

"If they won't listen to you now, Micah, what makes you think they're going to listen to you after even more time goes by?" I pressed him. "I mean, what if they actually end up following this guy, like, wherever he tells them to go? And you end up following *them*, and then you're all trapped in whatever this South Compound turns out to be?"

He kept shaking his head, like, *I don't know, I don't know.* That's when I got scared. Really scared. It was a shiver that flashed through me, like, this shit's real. And I know a lot about survival, but I don't know how you haul someone back when their mind's being controlled. It was clear that Micah knew—even if he didn't consciously understand it— that his parents had gone beyond the pale. That was our term for it: gone beyond the pale. Side note: his parents *were* pale at that point, literally. They were pale and thin and quiet. They weren't like that before, when I used to spend more time with them, before the blind potato eyes took over underground.

I mean, the Stones were board-game players. Old-school games like Risk and Scrabble and Monopoly. They would open a bottle of wine and pour a glass for all of us, even though Micah and I were underage—Micah is still underage—and play music and games late into the night. When I look back now, it's like a Hallmark card in my mind, if Hallmark made cards for holidays called Family Game Night. The Stones were so happy playing games. What made them *stop?*

The fact that they just let go of that happiness and sank themselves into the Prophet's bullshit scares the shit out of me. No, wait. "Scares" isn't the word. It infuriates the shit out of me. Micah tried to tread a fine line. On the one hand he was all, *The Prophet never fails to astound with his predictability,* and *It's like he read a book called* How to Become the Leader of a Stereotypical Cult, and on the other hand he was like, *Don't call them a cult, Ses. That's insulting to actual cults.*

Micah and I used to think that at some point things with the Prophet would get really serious, and then we would have to do something. We would have to be prepared. But looking back, we didn't prepare at all. We weren't ready.

It was kind of the same situation with my grandmother, too. I noticed that she was walking slower, that it was hard for her to climb the stairs to our apartment, but I brushed it aside. She must have sensed something wrong inside her, like she must have felt how hard it was to breathe, and how hard her heart was working, but she never said anything. Maybe neither of us wanted to worry.

What my grandmother died of: congestive heart failure by way of pneumonia, which I didn't even know she had. Pneumonia that began as a cough that we ignored. Pneumonia that took root in her.

How she died: quickly.

How she prepared me for her death: not at all.

You learn a lot when your sole caregiver dies. Some of the things you learn are logistic.

1. If you're under eighteen and your primary caregiver dies and you don't have any other living relatives and you can't stand the thought of living in a foster home, then you'd better be convincing when you conjure up a pretend aunt to take care of you.

2. It's way easier to be convincing than you thought it would be, like even with your best friends, who when you told them you were living with your aunt and she didn't allow any visitors, just accepted it.

3. You will receive Social Security survivor's money every month.

4. Your grandmother's belongings are now yours.

5. Rent is expensive.

6. If you're on a month-to-month lease, your landlord can terminate your lease with thirty days' notice and you'll quickly need to find a place to live.

7. It's not easy to find a place to live, because of the whole pretend-aunt thing.

8. You might have to make your own place to live.

9. Which you can do.

Some of the things you learn are about yourself.

1. You didn't know you would miss her so much.

2. You wish you had known she was about to die.

3. You didn't know how alone it would feel.

4. You didn't know what it would be like to walk up the stairs into that apartment above the cobbler for the first time after she died and hear only the faint noises from Soren instead of your grandmother, moving around in the kitchen, and realize that . . .

5. She wasn't there.

6. She wasn't going to be there.

7. Ever again.

Anyway.

It's not easy to find an apartment on your own when you're sixteen. Ever hear the terms "credit check" and "first and last" and "security deposit"? They all mean the same thing, which is money, which even with Social Security I didn't have nearly enough of. Even if I had a full-time job, which I didn't, I wouldn't have been able to afford even a one-room apartment.

The first two weeks, I slept at Inky's house. Her parents came to my grandmother's memorial service, which was held in Saint Paul, in the cafeteria of the school she'd worked in. Some of her coworkers from the cafeteria stood up and sang "Amazing Grace." Everyone brought potluck. We ate off paper plates with plastic forks. I remember some of this. The rest of it Inky and Sebastian told me.

Everyone at the service was kind and sad. Everyone at the service shook my hand and told me how sorry they were.

I hate thinking about it. I try not to think about it.

"When does your aunt get to town?" Inky's dad asked me. I had already spread the story about my aunt moving here from California to take care of me.

"Two weeks."

"Do you want to stay with us until she gets here, *mija*?"

Inky's mom asked. "I mean, if it would be easier than staying at your apartment"—*without your grandmother there*, was the rest of the sentence, but she didn't say it. I hesitated. My grandmother and I had always lived on our own together, and shouldn't I be able to live on my own? But it was also true that the thought of being back in our apartment without her was awful.

"Okay," I said. "Thank you."

Inky has a blow-up mattress in her room. We dragged it out from under her bed and blew the dust off it. For the two weeks I was there, I didn't sleep. Inky's ceiling is covered with glow-in-the-dark stars, a remnant from when she was a baby, and I lay there and traced the constellations with my eyes. Orion, Cassiopeia, and the Big Dipper are the only ones I knew, and they must be the only ones that Inky's parents knew, because they were the only constellations up there. The rest of the ceiling is covered with random stars and crescent moons, and my eyes went from one to another while I thought and thought and thought about where I would live.

And then I figured it out.

There are a lot of abandoned houses in Minneapolis—in any city, probably—and I conjured a sixth sense for where they were. When you focus hard on something, you develop a sixth sense for it. Like if there's a person you want or a person you're trying to avoid, you suddenly find signs of that person everywhere. You can sense the trail of their existence from classroom to cafeteria to sidewalk. Your senses are heightened in a specific and particular way.

Same thing with abandoned houses. Once your goal is to find a good one, you zero in. Here are some clues: (1) grass or weeds higher than at the surrounding houses, (2) trash in the yard, (3) front steps that are worn down and/or broken, (4) a porch, or front door hanging awry or slightly open, (5) a porch filled with things, like chairs, that look broken, (6) windows partially obscured with boards or stacks of boxes.

There are more abandoned houses than you'd think.

But an abandoned house wasn't what I wanted. What I wanted was a garage that belonged to an abandoned house. Because garages tend to be unnoticed. Garages line alleys, and alleys don't have sidewalks, with neighbors watching you walk in and out.

If a house is abandoned, then its garage will also be abandoned. And a garage is a kind of house. People in other countries think of the United States as a place so rich that people build houses for their cars. When you think about it, they're kind of right.

I'm not rich, but I guess I kind of am. Because I have a house that I live in for free.

My house is a single-wide garage in the East Calhoun neighborhood. I will not tell you exactly where it is. My house doesn't look like it's well-made—it's covered with vines and the paint is peeling—but it is. It's insulated, for one thing. It's made of cement blocks covered with insulated green-painted boards. Its roof is made of tin, which is unusual in the Midwest, where asphalt shingles rule. The roof has a skylight. When it rains, the rain drums down and I love the sound. Micah loved the sound too. On the nights he ~~stayed~~ *stays* at my house with me, we lie in bed and listen to the rain.

Who would put a skylight in a garage? Who would insulate the roof, and the walls? What kind of person does that? Someone who cared, that's who. Whoever made my garage-house put care and time and attention into it. They built it to last, and last it has.

The good thing about having a big pink apartment building next to my house is that I can walk freely up and down my alley. The apartment building is ugly—two and a half stories, the half story buried half underground and half above, the way a lot of apartment buildings are here, and pink, I mean, *pink?*—but it's also beautiful because of the cover it gives me. Directly across the alley is the back of a large office building, windowless and brick. The big garage door of my house fronts the alley, but you can't roll it up because the track is broken. The only way in and out of my house is through the service door, and the service door is hidden from view by the fence next to the apartment building.

I can slip through the narrow passageway between the shed—where they keep the apartment building's lawn mower and snowblower and other equipment—and the back wall of my house. I can slip along the side of the fence from the street and cut across the service walk. Or I can walk down the alley to the apartment building, then along the fence, and cut to my door through the abandoned house's yard. Multiple means of entry and exit.

Everyone thinks I live in the apartment building. Which makes sense. People are always moving in and out of big apartment buildings, and this pink one has dozens of units. Studio, one-bedroom, two-bedroom, and each one an I-can't-afford-it unit. Every month the vacancy sign out front changes, according to who's moving out and what's opening up. Everyone who sees me walking up and down the alley thinks I live there with a mom or a dad or some other relative who's older than me and is looking out for me. Like Tom, the guy who always stands outside the fourplex six doors down from the apartment building and across the alley, smoking.

"Hey, Shelly."

"Hey, Tom."

Tom is a true smoker. Dedicated to the cause. Rain, snow, sleet, heat, he's out. Micah and I call him Tom the Guy. He's young. Youngish anyway. When I walk past him, I picture his lungs inside his body as grayish, not fat and pink the way the lungs of a youngish person should be. Watch the way a true smoker sucks in the smoke and breathes out the smoke and bends over to hack. Listen to the rasp in their voice, the way their laugh catches and splits in two on the upswing. Now imagine their lungs. Grayish and slender.

Tom the Guy thinks my name is Shelly and I let him. Shelly. Esme. Emmy. These are some of the names people think I am. Either people don't listen too well, or they hear what they want to hear. Maybe both.

I furnished my house for free. Micah and I call it curbing. It's best to go curbing at the very end of the month, because that's when renters' leases are up and when people move in and out of their houses and apartments. It's also best to go curbing in a wealthy neighborhood, but wealth isn't necessary. Poor people put plenty of things out in the trash too.

Something to sleep on, a mattress or a bed or a futon. Pots and pans and dishes. Blankets and pillows. Bookcases. A fan or a space heater. Quilts and blankets and afghans and more quilts and blankets to nail up to the walls for more insulation. And for pretty, because quilts nailed to all the walls of a house are pretty. Winter boots, a summer dress, art supplies, a laundry basket, a five-gallon bucket to set beneath the leak in your roof. Everything in the world is findable.

Most things I found myself. Some of them, like the Amish star quilt and the electric fireplace, the one that looks like a real fireplace with real flames but that's actually a plug-in space heater, Micah found for me.

But how does she get electricity?

There are outdoor outlets everywhere. Some people don't even know they have outdoor outlets because they're camouflaged under painted hinged covers that swing up.

Outdoor extension cords come in all different colors and they are more easily hidden than you'd think. I have two, a white one for winter and a green one for summer. Both plug into the hard-to-find outlet on the side of the apartment building's storage shed. No one would notice the little bit of electricity I use, given how big the apartment building is, but I use it sparingly anyway. I'm trying to be a good neighbor.

But where does she go to the bathroom?

What does she do for water?

How does she stay clean? Does *she stay clean?*

If you're picturing a filthy girl in a filthy hut drinking out of a five-gallon pail filled with rainwater, don't. There's this thing called the YWCA, with endless toilets and showers, and it's five blocks away. And there's Lunds grocery store and a bunch of coffee shops within a couple of blocks if you need a bathroom. A pail behind a curtain does the job the rest of the time. As for drinking water, anyone can buy a jug of water anywhere. People think it's not possible that a teenager can live on her own and maintain any semblance of normalcy. But people are wrong.

What if your grandmother raised you to be vigilant, to protect yourself, to not ask for help? What if you're resourceful and self-sufficient and you have two good friends and a fake aunt and a tutoring job and a dog-walking job and plans for your future? What if the truth is that you don't want to live with anyone but your grandmother, ever?

That was me—resourceful and self-sufficient, with a job and friends and plans for my future—until Micah turned up in the alley. That was the day I realized how lonely I had been, ever since my grandmother died. Because Micah made the loneliness go away. Micah recognized me as a kindred spirit the very first time he came upon me. Micah held me all night long when I was cold, made me chicken soup in a curbside pot on my two-burner hot plate when I was sick, never told my two best friends where I lived because he knew it was secret, stayed up all night with me talking about the café we were going to open together after we graduated.

SESAME!

PRESENT TENSE!

Holds, makes, tells, knows, stays, are.

This whole time I've been thinking about cults and potatoes and my grandmother and the memorial service and not asking for help and staying vigilant and protecting myself, I have been walking. Walking and searching. Three white vans, all of which have car seats in them, all of which have BABY ON BOARD signs hanging in the windows. Two abandoned buildings, one of which is too dilapidated for habitation, and the other of which has no signs of life whatsoever. The vents of both of which I crouch next to and call into over and over, just to make sure. Anyone looking at me probably thinks I'm out searching for a lost pet.

"Micah!"

"MICAH!"

No answer.

Doesn't matter.

He's out there. I will find him.

11

Micah

Notes from the Underground

When conducting formal or informal scientific research, you begin by posing a question. Then you set the parameters of both the question and your subject of inquiry, design a study, figure out how to conduct your study, analyze your data, and arrive at a conclusion. Direct observation is a scientific method available to anyone. I'm using it to conduct my own informal scientific research on the Living Lights.

> QUESTION: How long will it take for one person to persuade seventeen other people to follow him into the earth and do exactly as he says?

PLACE AND TIME OF STUDY: A major metropolitan area—the Twin Cities, located in the far north of the middle of the country—in the first quarter of the twenty-first century.

STUDY METHOD: Observe the person along with everyone he draws to himself, including your parents, yourself, and the other fourteen members of the Living Lights. Keep an ongoing log of notes until either (a) seventeen people head below the ground or (b) they don't.

CONCLUSION: Seventeen people in a major metropolitan area will follow a person below the ground and do exactly as he says in approximately four years.

The prophet and Deeson warn me that when I get to zero, the congregation will be obliged to cast me out of eden. Which is another word the prophet uses. Being cast out of eden sounds kind of good at first, like maybe it means being kicked out of Living Lights, which, great. But the way they say it scares me. There's something sinister in their voices.

See what I'm doing here? Lowercase instead of upper.

> prophet
> acolyte
> eden

It has become clear that to the prophet anything other than abject loyalty and obedience is an infraction, and I'm his chief rebel. I'm his *only* rebel. "Question not." "Ask not." "Protest not." Deeson has taken to talking like that. The order of language itself is being changed around down here in the gathering of the Living Lights.

If it sounds like a reality show, it feels like one, only without the funny. Call it *White-Robed and Afraid*. Call it *Meet the Living Lights*. Call it *Get Me the Fuck Out of Here*.

Eleven adults sleep on cots in the Men's and Women's Rooms of Sleep. Six children, all but one of whom are under the age of ten, sleep on cots in the Boys' and Girls' Rooms of Sleep. The only person who sleeps alone is me. I used to sleep in a closet but now, because of infractions, I sleep in the laundry room. *We* sleep in the laundry room. If I call myself We, I feel stronger. We are legion. We contain multitudes. We can sleep in a corner of the laundry room. We don't even mind it, because you know why? There's a screened vent in the laundry room, and beyond the darkness there must be light. There must be air. There must be the world above.

Both my data and my conclusions are unimpeachable. They were conducted via intimate, real-life observation over a long time, and I can verify what happened at every step of the way. What I did not expect is what happened just now, when I summarized my scientific observations.

I felt sick. I *feel* sick.

Not just because I'm scared that somehow Deeson or the prophet will sense me thinking these thoughts in my head through the locked laundry room door and come storming in. Not because my points are disappearing, due to infractions transgressed by me. Is "transgressed" a word? It is now, Ses. Not because Jerald and Krystyna have singled me out the same way Deeson and the prophet have singled me out, and are turning the little kids against me. I hear them whispering about me.

"Micah," is all Jerald has to say, and Krystyna smirks.

And then all the little kids smirk. I look at them and they all look back at me as though I'm an object of scorn. As though they want nothing to do with me. *Hey, Krystyna, I want to say, remember when you told me why you changed your name? Because you didn't want to be associated with the mean girl?*

I don't say anything, though. What good would it do? More points would be taken away, is all.

Here's why I feel sick: because I'm hungry. I've never been hungry this long before, Ses. Have you? Maybe when your grandmother died, you were this hungry.

My parents are with the others. They are not locked up. I know this because my mom whispered through the locked door.

"Micah, it's Mom," she said in this tiny, scared voice. "Dad and I are worried about you. Micah, you have to obey the rules here. Please, honey. Behave, and they'll let you out."

My parents, they used to be so normal. Typical. My mom was the produce manager at Cub Foods and my dad was a receptionist at the dentist three blocks away. Regular jobs with regular paychecks and we lived/live in a regular house and we did regular things like have a firefly-themed birthday party. And within four years neither of my parents have a job and we live underground.

It's like you're living one life, and then suddenly you wake up and you're in a whole new world. You look back on the old life and it comes into your mind in flashes all filled with sunlight, like even if you didn't think you were always happy, now you think, *I was so happy*. And the life you're in now is cold and small and narrow and cement and the only way out is to get beamed up on a shaft of light.

They still try to act like parents sometimes. Like my mom, when she whispered through the door that I should behave. And yesterday, or whenever it was—I don't know what day it is anymore—when they let me out for Reflection and she saw my hands. "Micah, what happened to your hands?" with this worried tone in her voice. "Laundry," I said. "Cold water." I would have said more, but she put her hands over mine and patted them and I choked up. It was like for a minute she was my mom, my *real* mom instead of a pale woman in a white robe. You know? Then Deeson saw her holding my hands and shook his head and frowned and she let go.

It's like she forgot for a minute that her brain has been overrun by the prophet, and her normal parent reflexes kicked in. Like if your car battery's almost dead but when you turn the key the engine still tries to ignite. The engine and the battery and the carburetor and the ignition remember what they're supposed to do and who they're supposed to be, but they can't get back there. They're stuck forever, half remembering what their purpose in life was.

My mom blinked and looked away. Short-circuited by Deeson. There's a routine down here, at least for everyone else who's not locked in the laundry room, and it never varies: rise, make your cot, breakfast, do chores, adults to Adult Room of Reflection and children to Children's Room of Reflection, lunch, chores, Reflection, chores, dinner, Reflection, chores, bed. Whatever we used to do in our aboveground homes doesn't matter. It's the prophet channel now, and what the prophet decrees is what everyone does.

My parents are in their forties, but they're fading. They barely remember the world of sunlight and the people they used to be, who had regular jobs and regular school and regular everything. Fuck that! Fuck them! Fuck you, prophet!

Shhh. Stop. That's me, telling myself to be quiet, to not let them see how I really feel. Because what good does it do? We're down here and we're stuck, and my parents can't go back and undo everything they did and didn't do.

How long has it been now, Ses? A week? More? I've lost

track. I'm trying to remind myself that there's a real world up there, and you're in it. You're real in the real world. Aren't you?

Sesame, are you there? Can you hear me?

Ses, it's hard to be down here. It's hard to be surrounded by seventeen people who believe that Living Lights is the divine path and the prophet is the only one who can lead them on that path and that abandonment of the secular world is the only way to be a Living Light.

You know what's funny, even though it's not? That the project is Living Light, but we're actually living in a windowless basement.

Strive to be worthy, Micah, the prophet says. In the beginning I used to tell him I was striving.

I'm striving, prophet, I'm striving. Seriously striving.

That's what I used to tell him. Remember when I used to laugh about him, about his eyes, the way they went flat? Sesame, why did I laugh? I'm trying to remember what I thought was funny about it. Maybe because I could get away back then? Maybe because I used to talk right back at him, laugh at him and then run away to you?

Jesus, Sesame, was I that stupid? Did I really believe he was a nothing, that anyone could see through him, that in the end he was a laughingstock?

Because here's the thing, Ses: no one sees through him here except me.

Remember how in the beginning we used to laugh at him at night, how I used to walk around like him and repeat the things he used to say the way he used to say them? You said I was a great mimic. "Be the prophet, Micah," you used to say. We'd laugh and laugh, only quietly, so that if someone was walking down the alley, they wouldn't hear us and call the cops.

Here's a question for you. How does someone get to be a capital-*P* Prophet? How does one ordinary person decide that he's not ordinary, and then how does he suck those around him into believing he's special? That he has information and power that the rest of us don't? Maybe it's a force field. Maybe a human being can create some kind of invisible force field around himself and suck others in because power over others is what matters to them.

And who's more powerful than God, right? If you believe in God, I mean.

And next to God, who's the most powerful? The one who channels the word of God.

Enter the P/prophet.

The P/prophet wants his own Wikipedia page. I overheard him tell Deeson. He said "my own Wikipedia page," as though having your own Wikipedia entry was an unheard-of level of accomplishment. He probably wants it listed under the Prophet instead of his real name, which is Ronald Gasberger.

Are you laughing out there, in your secret house? Did I just make you laugh? Wasn't me, Ses, it was Ronnie. That's his actual name. Kid you not. He used to go by Ronnie, back in the early days of the Living Lights.

Fuck him. I'm going to call him the prft.

Hear the difference? Prophet. prophet. prft.

Don't feel sorry for the prft because he was once a little kid with the name Ronald Gasberger. Or, okay, feel sorry for him, because it's a terrible name. But doesn't everyone in the world have something awful that hurts them? Someone laughing at their ridiculous name, or their clothes, or their hair, or their body, or their whatever? But that awfulness doesn't make them believe they should control the destinies of humankind, does it? No. Except a few, like the prft.

See? It's good for me to talk to you in my head. By the time I'm done talking with you, the Prophet has shrunk into the prft.

It has been a long time since I ate, Sesame. I've lost track of how long. I tell myself to be quiet, but I can't stop. Like yesterday, or last night, whenever it was, when Deeson unlocked the laundry room door and let me out for Reflection. They were all waiting for me. All the white-robed Lights lined up single file in the hallway, blinking under the fluorescent lights. Silent, even the kids. Krystyna and Jerald made faces at me when the adults weren't looking, which made all the other kids start to laugh. Not a good laugh, though. Mean. Nasty.

Fuck this.

"prft?"

He wheeled around and glared at me. Deeson smirked.

I could feel the tension in all of them. They were all waiting for me to transgress again.

"Stone."

"I'm curious. Why 'Room of Reflection' instead of 'Reflection Room'?"

Just a simple, ordinary question, right? Just asking, right? Except not, because everyone, even me, could hear the disdain in my voice. He pounced almost before I had finished asking the question.

"Insubordination! Minus five points!"

I am down to forty-five points. My parents don't want me to use up all my points. They don't want me to get to zero. The thing is, I keep infracting. The other thing is, I'm not trying to infract. It's like whatever I say or do is an infraction. It's like whatever *they* do is an infraction too. Like my mom, sneaking out of the Room of Reflection to go to the bathroom but instead sneaking down the hall to the laundry room again and whispering my name under the door.

Micah?

Mom? Is that you?

Both of us in tiny voices.

Yes, honey. It's me. How are you? Are you hungry?

Kind of.

Did they give you the bowl of rice last night, Micah? I sacrificed the—

But then there were footsteps, heavy ones, and my mom was surrounded. I could feel it. Then I could hear it.

WHAT ARE YOU DOING NO ONE GAVE YOU THE RIGHT TO NO ONE SAID YOU COULD

And that was it. They took her back down the hall. She tried, though. My mom tried. As for the bowl of rice she was talking about, no. I don't know what she sacrificed for that bowl of rice, but I never got it.

Take away his phone, take away his points, take away his food, take away his parents, take away his life.

There is a potato hidden behind the vent screen.

I am saving the potato in case things get dire.

I stole it from the kitchen in the middle of the night when Deeson forgot to lock the door to the laundry room. *Moving like a cat, the young transgressor slipped from his cot in utter darkness and made his way by memory and feel to the kitchen, where a bin of potatoes awaited peeling the next day. Soundlessly, the transgressor lifted the lid and removed a single potato, which he secreted in his underwear, and made his way back to his cot.*

Yeah. You read that right. The potato made its way back to the laundry room in my underwear. Desperate times, Ses. We'll laugh about it someday. I promise. I promise you we'll laugh. Remember how much we laughed, Ses? Like that one night in your house when we named the mosquito Jameson because we were drinking Jameson and then we started matching pitch with Jameson's whine and then we started toasting him? There was a lot of toasting. There was a lot of laughing.

Remember I cooked you dinner earlier at my house? Ravioli with smoked mushrooms and wilted greens and cold radishes dipped in cold butter. Radishes and butter and salt. My God I'm hungry.

We are somewhere in a city, Sesame. There are sirens and there are dogs and there is a potato hidden behind a screened vent.

I stood on top of the laundry tub and pried the screen out with my fingernails and a shard of plastic that came from the lid of my toilet bucket. How it got to be a shard is I jumped on it until it broke. There's darkness behind the screen vent, and the smell is stale and moldy, but it must lead to the world above. It must because it must. Which is tautological reasoning, but like I said, Sesame, desperate times. The plan was I would go with my parents to watch out for them, to get us out of wherever the Prophet was taking us, but I see now how stupid I was to think we could just leave whenever we wanted. All the doors to the world above are locked. There's no way out of this place. For me, or for my parents.

The prft has a headlamp now. It's on all the time. He walks around and inspects the rooms and the kitchen and the bathrooms by angling his head so that his headlamp shines in all the corners. You can't look at him directly anymore because the light is blinding. It's one of those bike headlamps with different modes: (1) steady, (2) blinking, (3) wild flashing. Maybe he keeps it on steady or blinking and only switches it to wild flashing for me, when he lets me out of the laundry room. I don't know. I haven't asked, because I'm down to forty-five points and every question I ask, I lose another five.

> Prft: "Look at me, Micah."

> Me: (*Fuck you.*) "I am, prft."

> Prft: "You are not."

> Me: (*Fuck you.*) "I am, prft."

> Prft: "Are you arguing with me?"

> Me: (*Fuck you.*) "No, prft."

These little conversations happen after evening Reflection. The adult Living Lights begin to gather right around the second time I say, "I am." Deeson's usually in front, with the look on his face that I think of as his prft smirk. Wife is in back. The Ms, Fallon and Gregory, who are knitters, are behind him. They can knit standing up now, in the dark. They don't even look down at what they're knitting. What *are* they knitting, anyway? No clue.

> Prft: "Have you conjugated your purpose in the afterlife today, Micah?"

Me: (*Conjugate means to join together
in pairs, prft. Or to recite the different
forms of a verb in a particular order.*)
"Do you mean have I *contemplated*
my purpose in the afterlife today,
prft?"

This is where you can feel the air in the room change.
It happens instantaneously. This is why the Living Lights
gather to watch when the prft shines his light on me. They
come reluctantly, but in their reluctance there's also a
willingness. They're spectators at a bullfight, and I am the
bull. The knitters keep right on knitting, and Deeson keeps
right on smirking, and Wife huddles by the side wall with
her white robe partly pulled up like she's trying to hide
something just below her neck—a scar? A cut? A bruise?
And my parents are by now hovering at the back of the
gathering, because the expected has happened. Micah has
challenged the prft.

Did I?

Is that what my question was, a challenge?

It's cold in the laundry room, Ses. It's damp. It's hard
to get warm. Sometimes I do jumping jacks in the middle
of the night if I can't stop shivering. That works. For a
while.

What happened was we left the world of sun and light
and we descended two flights of stairs into the belly of the
beast. Here we are gathered together to fight the armies

of darkness. Which is ironic, because when the prft talks about the armies of darkness, everything he talks about is aboveground, in the world of sun and light. He doesn't see how dark it is down here. Literally it's dark—all the floor lamps are gone now, and we're down to bare bulbs overhead—and it's dark in our minds. People are quiet now. There's a lot of sleeping. When it's quiet and dark, your body wants to sleep. Or maybe it's your mind that wants to sleep. To get away. It's dark and heavy here in the underworld, and there is no lightness.

The prft's reach is long. He is gaining power as I think these thoughts.

Everything is foreboding.

12

Sesame

MY NEW ROUTINE has taken over.

Sleep, sort of, as much as I can anyway between worrying and checking my phone.

Get up before daybreak.

Check the phone again.

Call Officer Emmanuel: "Hi, Officer Emmanuel, it's Sesame Gray. I'm calling about my boyfriend, Micah Stone. There's still no word and it's been six days/seven days/eight/nine days." She won't reopen the case, but when winter break ends and he doesn't show up at Southwest, I want Micah's name to be instantly familiar.

Go to the Jameses to pick up more flyers. James Two

makes fifty copies every day in the copy room at work and leaves them for me on their porch bench so I can pick them up anytime, day or night.

Go to Greenway Elementary and write poems with Vong. Today is the last day of school before winter break, then winter break begins. I haul out my ID at the front desk on the way in, like always, and like always, I wait for Miss Najma, the secretary, to print out my ID badge. I sign in, I peel off the adhesive backing, I stick the badge onto my jacket.

"Everything okay, Sesame?"

Miss Najma is looking at me with concern. She's known me for a long time now, ever since I got this tutoring job.

"You're pretty quiet these days," she continues. "You seem a little anxious."

"Everything's fine," I say, but this doesn't seem to satisfy her, so I cast about for something else. "It's just so cold," I add. "Hard to get warm."

At this, Miss Najma smiles. That's the thing about living in Minneapolis. You can always rely on the weather for a distraction. The truth is that everything about this daily check-in process is annoying. Miss Najma knows exactly who I am, and so does everyone else I pass on the way to the Greenway Elementary tutoring room, which is right off the main office, yet I still have to go through this charade of ID, sign in, badge.

But a cult can take someone away and no one even notices. It scares the shit out of me.

"For real," Miss Najma agrees. "It's a good thing we're tough, right? And a double good thing that as of tomorrow we're officially on break, right?"

Right.

Vong is waiting for me in the reading room. He taps his giant wristwatch when I walk in. He's added another rubber band to the two he keeps wound around it. It's doubtful Vong will ever be big enough to fit that wristwatch. But I'll say this, the kid is always on time. He tilts his head and gives me a questioning look. I shake my head.

"No word," I say. "The search continues."

Vong frowns. He opens his notebook and pulls out another poem.

> Micah Stone
> where have you flown
> we are alone
> since you have gone
> please come back

"The last lines don't rhyme," he says.

"Actually, 'gone' does rhyme," I say. "Even if it doesn't *sound* like 'alone' and 'flown,' it's still an official rhyme because its ending is the same as 'gone.' Now, 'please come back' isn't exactly a rhyme, but—"

I stop. I'm trying to shift into writing tutor mode, someone knowledgeable about the differences between rhyming poetry and free verse, but it's not working.

Because who cares? Vong's poem is exactly how I feel. Micah has flown and I am alone since he has gone. I am alone, I am alone, I am alone. I close my eyes. Then I feel a clunk on my hand. Vong is trying to hold my hand—this tiny little second grader—but the giant wristwatch gets in the way.

"Thanks, buddy," I say. "I love this poem. I'll add it to the stack."

When the hour is up, I tell Vong I'll see him after break. And then I continue the search.

If I find an abandoned building, I walk around it with a long stick. I poke it down every vent I see, every crack. Bend down and cup my hands around my mouth and call through the vents and cracks. "Micah! MICAH! Hello! Hellooooo! Anyone in there?" Walk until I'm too cold to walk anymore, then go inside a coffee shop and warm up until I can walk again.

Keep going. Staple flyers up to every pole. Restock every poem box with flyers. Collect any notes left behind and add them to the stack of Micah Christmas notes on the poems table in my house.

You don't know me, but we are all praying for Micah to come home soon!

THANK YOU FOR ALL THE POEMS. I'M ASHAMED I NEVER LEFT YOU A NOTE BEFORE. THANK YOU AND JUST SO YOU KNOW, I HOPE HE COMES HOME SOON.

Poem Person, is Micah your boyfriend? Your brother? Your son? Whoever he is, he looks like such a nice and good person. My biggest hope is that next time I come to get a poem from this box, I will see a note that says Micah is home!!!!!

When the sun goes down, I meet Inky and Sebastian in the library conference room. They'll start searching with me when break starts tomorrow. Right now they're constantly monitoring the Missing Micah Instagram and Facebook and Twitter accounts they set up on the first night. They are both administrators, and one of them responds to everyone who writes in, whether it's a credible tip or not. Not that there have been any credible tips. They would let me know instantly if there were, so there's no real need to meet in person, but we do anyway. Because they are my best friends. Because Inky always has a cappuccino for me. Because Sebastian somehow can make me smile no matter what.

Go to the Y. Work out. Shower. Dress. Go home.

Try to sleep.

Dawn. Time to get up, even though it's Saturday.

I check my phone: nothing. Time to make my call. Whoa! She picks up! Isn't it too early for her to be at her desk? Then I remind myself it's a police station. They're always open.

"Hello, Officer Emmanuel, it's Sesame."

"Hi, Sesame." Her voice is friendly and calm. She must

be used to me and my daily voice mails by now. "Do you have new information for me?"

"Not really. I was just wondering—"

"If anyone else has called in a missing person report? I can't comment on that. But I can tell you that we have received nothing pertinent to your situation."

"Are you *sure*?" I say this so she'll have to think twice, just in case anything has slipped her mind.

"I'm sure. If we do receive information that makes us reopen the case, I'll let you know immediately. Keep in touch."

There's a tiny hint of a smile in her voice when she says, "Keep in touch." Probably because she knows I'll be in touch. I'm always in touch. I call her every day. Maybe I'm driving Officer Emmanuel crazy, but you know what? I don't care. Next, I put on all my layers and head over to the Jameses' house to collect more flyers. Today they're up, drinking their coffee, waiting for me with a full to-go mug. The Jameses' coffee isn't a cappuccino from Inky, but I'm grateful to them. They are always kind. James One hands me my coffee, and James Two hands me the envelope full of new flyers, copied covertly at his office.

"I called Officer Emmanuel myself yesterday," James One says.

"You *did*?" The surprise in my voice makes him smile.

"Yep. Just to keep her on her toes. Let her know we're on Team Sesame."

Aha. Maybe that's why she picked up when I called this

morning. "Officer Emmanuel says to let her know if new information comes in," I say. "The minute she knew about the school excuse, she quit caring, though. Case closed."

"Nothing from Inky and Sebastian?"

I shake my head.

"Your aunt back yet?"

Again I shake my head. They ask every day, in person or via text. They've searched Micah's parents' names in the special professional databases available to them at their jobs: nothing. They've called all the area hospitals just in case a seventeen-year-old male John Doe's been brought in. What a scary but great idea. Why didn't I think of it myself?

"No news, though," James Two says. "We're sorry, Sesame."

Their kindness makes it even worse that I'm lying to them about my aunt. I hate lying to the Jameses. Or lying about anything to anyone, including Inky and Sebastian. Lying to keep your life intact and whole is one thing, lying by omission is another. But I'm not going to tell them I live alone.

Then James One puts his hand on my shoulder and my throat closes up.

I will myself not to cry.

Prince and Peabop are looking at me sadly, both their tails wagging in unison, and suddenly I get an idea. How, how, how had I not thought of this before?

"Hey," I say. "Would it be okay if I took Prince and

Peabop with me while I look for the South Compound?"

"Of course," the Jameses say simultaneously, and James Two says, "Why didn't *I* think of that? It's a great idea."

"Give them a T-shirt to sniff," James One says. "Or a few of them. Anything with Micah's scent on it."

"And explain to them what you want them to do," James Two says. "They're not trained search dogs, but they're smart. On some level, they'll understand."

"We'll join you tomorrow," James One says, and then, at a look from James Two, he adds, "If he hasn't turned up by then, I mean. Which we hope he will."

It's December in Minneapolis, ten days into this siege. Take your pick of hypothermia, starvation, dehydration: any of them can kill. *Don't be dramatic, Sesame,* I tell myself, but in my bones I know I'm not being dramatic. I'm being realistic.

"Meanwhile, I'll make a bunch more flyers at work today, since it's Saturday and no one else will be there," James Two says. "Enough to get us through a few days at least." He gives me a sneaky smile. Maybe he likes being a rule breaker.

When I walk into the conference room, Inky and Sebastian are already there. The momentary relief I felt from the Jameses' kindness earlier dissolves instantly, because the air in the room is flat. Inky and Sebastian look tired. I'm tired too—I've been out in the cold for four hours already—but I force myself to smile. Today is the first day of winter break, and they're taking the afternoon to help me search, and I feel both grateful and guilty.

"Thanks, you two," I say, and they both nod.

"People are leaving notes in the poem boxes," I say, like this will somehow renew their energy. "I'm saving them all as a Christmas present for Micah. A homecoming present."

They nod again. Inky's brought me a cappuccino. Extra cinnamon, extra froth, extra tall. "Sesquipedalian" is the name she's written on it. That's a new one. She wrote it carefully, each letter separated by a little space, which means she had to look it up.

"Know what sesquipedalian means?" she says, and I shake my head. "A foot and a half," she says, measuring with her hands.

"Now, isn't that useful," Sebastian says. "Super useful."

I know they're trying, trying to drum up energy, trying to act normal. They don't want me to see that they are losing hope, but I know them too well. They have come into the conference room trailing dark threads of anxiety and frustration. The air is thick with invisible stress. This has to change. I take a deep breath.

"So, I thought of a great idea," I say. "You know Peabop and Prince?"

They nod. Of course they know Peabop and Prince.

"We'll use them as search-and-rescue dogs," I say. "Give them something with the scent of Micah on it and tell them it's their job to find him. The Jameses think it's a great idea too."

"Their *job?*" Sebastian says. "Aren't Prince and Peabop, like, ordinary dogs?"

"Yeah," Inky says. "I mean, I don't want to be discouraging, but don't you have to be specially trained to be a search dog?"

"They *are* specially trained," I say. "They're *dogs*. And they love Micah."

Inky and Sebastian look at each other. They are communicating silently.

"It   is   worth   a   shot," I say, putting a tiny space between each word. They hear the tiny spaces and they rise to the occasion.

"Okay," Inky says, and "What do we have to lose?" Sebastian says, and "Point us in the right direction," Inky says, and out the door we go.

It's their first time at the Jameses' house, and Inky and Sebastian want to hang out there for a while because who wouldn't, but I wave my hand in the air like a conductor. *Allegro! Presto!* Once Peabop and Prince are clipped into their leashes and harnesses, we head out, straight to Micah's house.

"We have to go back in there?" Inky says, with a shiver.

"It's kind of creepy," Sebastian adds. "Don't you have anything of Micah's at your place?"

Yes, but no way we're going to my house.

"They need to smell Micah's things and also get a whiff of his parents," I say. "Because if they're all together, wherever they are, then that'll give the dogs a better chance."

Micah's house feels dead in the way that abandoned houses always feel. There's a certain feel to an empty building. A house needs people to feel alive. Otherwise the process of decay will begin. Micah's house is already decaying. There's a stain in the corner of the kitchen ceiling—an ice dam on the roof, slowly melting through the layers? There's a dark patch on the floor in front of the living room window—some kind of rodent leaving its mark? Dead bugs litter the stairs, and the air in the whole house feels cold and ungiving and angry. *You left us,* the house is saying to us. *Don't expect us to stay the same in your absence.*

It's awful being here.

We all feel it.

Inky and Sebastian stand silent and still by the kitchen counter, where the three phones are still lined up next to each other by the toaster. The phones are forbidding, but I pick Micah's up anyway and hold it in both hands. It's cold. A corpse of communication. I call up some of my favorite lines by my favorite poets, to try to give myself strength. "Let him enter the lion's cage." Danez Smith, poet warrior of Saint Paul, across the Mississippi River. Lucille Clifton and her poem about the waters rushing back, about being drowned, about drowning. What about Yeats? I wait for the right lines to come to me because Yeats always comes through, but what comes is "Yet we, for all that praise, could find nothing but darkness overhead," and they are not the right lines. Not, not, not the right lines.

Then I think of the right lines:

> *Roses are red*
> *violets are blue*
> *this poem is for you.*
> *I wish on the stars*
> *I wish on the moon*
> *that the boy who's gone*
> *comes home soon.*

Lines written not by a famous poet but by a stranger right here in South Minneapolis who's thinking of both Micah and me. Not half a mile away my house pulses with the presence of all the poems scrolled and waiting inside it. Scattered around the southwestern quadrant of the city are all the poem boxes, filled now with photos of Micah's smiling face and the notes people have left for me. For him. For us. I picture Vong and the poems he wrote for Micah. I picture all the other people out there who know that Micah's gone, who are worried about him, who are hoping and praying he comes home soon. The thought of those unknown people gives me strength.

"Let's go," I say, and I grab the leashes and charge upstairs to Micah's room. The air is as cold and still upstairs as down. Prince and Peabop prowl around to the end of their leashes, circling me, nosing each other, almost getting tangled.

"We're on a mission, boys," I say. "Stay with me now."

I pull open Micah's middle drawer, where he ~~kept~~ keeps his T-shirts, and lift a stack of them out. Most of them are bands, Minneapolis bands. Vintage ones like the Replacements and the Suicide Commandos and Soul Asylum and Babes in Toyland and Prince, all found at Value Village. Newer ones from shows we went to together, like Doomtree and Brother Ali and Atmosphere and Dessa. Holding them in my hands is like holding something living. It's like Micah is with us in that room.

Inky and Sebastian are coming up after us, slow feet on the stairs, whispering to each other, and I bury my head in the T-shirts to drown out the feeling of hesitation and reluctance that's coming with them. The T-shirts smell like him. He's here. We are breathing his air. *Micah, we will find you.*

"Here," I say to the dogs, and I kneel down beside them and hold the T-shirts out to them. They dip their heads down and snuff in the scent. They know what to do. Second by second, they turn serious and focused.

"Shaolin?"

It's Sebastian. He and Inky are standing in the door-way of Micah's room. I look up and around the room, seeing it the way they must be seeing it. They've never been in it before. Micah's bed, a mattress on the floor with a striped bottom sheet and no top sheet—Micah doesn't believe in top sheets—and a huge gray comforter he rolls himself up in like a sausage to sleep. Old *City Pages* covers taped around the wall. The dresser that I'm kneeling in front of. The closet with its door hanging open, shoes and boots and dirty clothes strewn around inside it. Except for the frozen dead air, Micah's room looks like an ordinary room that's lived in. A room that someone comes home to. A room that someone left one morning expecting to come back to that night. I rise from the floor and give a tug to the leash.

"Come on," I say. "He's somewhere out there. He's somewhere not far away. That's what I believe."

That's what I *have* to believe. But I don't say that.

13

Micah

IF THE WORDS are only in my head, is that still writing?
If I picture them as I say them, like lines running across my
notebook, does that count as invisible writing? What if I
forget what I'm pretend-writing? What if I forget what I'm
actually thinking?

These are the questions that run around my brain.
Rats chasing each other's tails. I watch them run and I
wish I could run. Sometimes I used to run to your house,
Sesame. It was 1.5 miles from my house to yours, an easy
run but still a run. Sometimes I made it a longer run by
running around Bde Maka Ska first, then veering off on
34th Street so I could stop at the Little Free Library there.

You know the one, on that dead-end street, so only walkers and runners pass by. The white one, with *Karma* painted on the side in blue letters.

Sometimes I carried your poems with me when I ran and I left them behind in the Karma library. You think the owner of the Karma library ever watched me from behind the window? You think they wonder why I haven't been by? You think they miss the poems? Because I do. I miss you reciting poems to me.

Here's something that happened.

Prft: "Room inspection."

Me: "What, we're military now?"

Prft: Silence. Walks into the
laundry room. Pokes at the
cinder blocks. Ducks his head
to see beneath the laundry tubs.
Peers behind them. Tries to push
them to one side so he can see
behind them, but they're heavy
and the prft's weak.

Me: "What are you looking for, prft?"

Prft: Silence. Turns his back to
me and tilts his head up at the

screened crawl space. (*Don't look there. Turn around. Look at me instead.*) Studies the dark and dirty frame of the crawl-space screen. Turns back to me. "Open that."

Me: "Open what?"

Prft: "That window."

Me: "It's not a window. It's a screen that covers the crawl space."

Prft: "Open it."

Me: "Why?"

Prft: Silence.

By this time others have gathered at the entrance to the laundry room. Little pale people all lumped up together, their big eyes staring through the doorframe. Little jeering children led by Krystyna and Jerald. In the back I see my mother. It kills me to look at my mother, my mother who was never quiet, never silent, but who is silent now. My mother who hugged me every day before I left for school because *I'm your mom and you are my only child and I love love love you, Micah Stone, got it?* My mother who took no shit from people, on the phone or at work or on the street. But look at her now, taking shit along with everyone else down here. She looks as scared as the others. No, she looks more scared than the others. Because her only child who she loves loves loves is in trouble. A geyser of anger boils up inside me. *If you love love love me so much, why don't you stand up for me, Mom?* Same for my father. *Why don't you call him out, Dad? You looked at me lately? No. You look every-where* but *at me. I'm your goddamn son.*

I keep losing points.

Eyes boring into me. It's a showdown. An MMA bout about to begin. One contestant's famished and dizzy, the other's stuffed with rice and potatoes and whatever other white food they're eating now in the rooms beyond the laundry room. I rise up on the balls of my feet and make my hands into fists. The prft's eyes flicker from my eyes to my feet and hands. I bounce a little, jog from foot to foot. The prft will be knocked out in the eighth round. Already he's losing ground in the face of my balled-up fists, my danc-ing feet. He's shrinking. The crawl-space screen will not be removed and my words will be safe. The notebook will stay hidden.

Lies.

Deeson pushes through the lump of scared watchers and stands between the prft, who's not shrunken at all, and me.

"I'll do it, Prophet," he says, and he looks at the prft, seeking approval. You can hear the difference between his Prophet and my prft. It's immediate and clear. The capital *P*, the rounded *o* and definite *t*. The way I say his name, it comes out in a crunched-up swallow, dark and ugly. The prft nods at Deeson and before the nod is finished, Deeson's hauled himself onto the laundry tub and is balancing on the edge with one hand pressed to the cinder-block wall to hold himself steady. The other hand claws at the screen and the whole screened frame comes right off the wall—because that's what I designed it to do—and the musty black interior gapes at us like a crypt.

"Inspect the interior," says the prft, like a fucked-up commander of a fucked-up branch of a dark militia, and Deeson pushes himself up on his toes and claws around the blackness with spread fingers, turning his head so he doesn't breathe in the moldy dust that comes wafting out.

"AHA," says Deeson, and his dusty clawed fingers bring forth my pencil.

So fucked up.

When did everything get so fucked up?

We all filed down into this basement and pulled the roof of the world over our heads.

How Hello Kitty and the potato escaped Deeson's clawing fingers I don't know, but they did. Maybe because Deeson's arms are shorter than mine, maybe because he can't stretch as far as me into the darkness, maybe because he wasn't looking for anything in particular, so when he found the pencil, he was stunned and thrilled to have found anything, anything at all besides dust. Hello Kitty and the potato might be covered with musty black dust and cobwebs, but they're still there. Vong's poem is still in the notebook, on the first page: *Roses are red, violets are blue, someday I'll write a poem TOO.*

Are you still out there, Vong? Still speaking in a British accent?

Here in my corner of the laundry room I hunch into a ball and set things up invisibly, only in my mind: my notebook, my pencil, and the *drip drip drip* of the white robes I washed this morning—or was it last night? or the afternoon? I don't know anymore—hanging from the white crisscrossing laundry lines above me. In my mind I hold the pencil lightly, the way they taught us to in elementary school. I bear down lightly on the paper, so I don't waste graphite. In my mind I write small, so I don't waste paper. Who knows when more of either pencil or paper will appear? Who knows how long we'll be down here? Who knows when my points will be gone? Who knows what will happen then?

Sesame.

Sesame.

Sesame.

Sometimes I say your name inside my head, and sometimes I say it out loud. Can you hear me? Sesame, I'm sorry. We had a plan and it got messed up. I didn't think it through. The situation felt like a joke. It *is* a joke, but it's a joke that could cost me everything. Sesame, I'm sorry. This must suck. You must be losing your mind, even if no one but maybe Inky and Sebastian know it. Are the three of you in the conference room right at this minute? Is it day or night out there? I listen for the sirens and the dogs, but sirens and dogs are all day and all night. How long have I been awake? Have I slept? It's hard to remember. When was the last time they fed me?

Jesus, Sesame, did you hear that? *When was the last time they fed me?* That is so, so different from *When was the last time I ate?*

First they took away my clothes.

Then they took away my cot.

Then they locked me in the laundry room.

Then they took away my food.

Then they took away my pencil.

Everything I do and say is an infraction. I heard my mother ~~asking pleading~~ begging the prft to let her give me some of her points.

"Not possible," the prft said. "You have no points. You are not on a points system. Micah is the only member on a points system. He gains and loses points on his own."

"How can he gain them, then?" my mother said. I could hear the franticness in her voice, humming below the pleading surface.

The prft didn't answer. Or at least I didn't hear him say anything. My mother can't donate her points to me

155

because she has no points to give. There is nothing to stop the erosion of mine.

What does it take to turn someone into a follower, Sesame?

What does it take to break someone who's *not* a follower?

Are these the only two choices?

If I knew whether it was day or night, that would make a difference. If I could sync myself up with the above world, or even with the Lightlys, who are going about their daily and nightly routines, that would make a difference. But the prft and Deeson have now cut off contact with the laundry room for anyone but them. Deeson comes every day and unlocks the door and delivers more dirty robes for me to wash, and then he locks the door again. It smells in here from cold and dirty laundry, and the waste bucket in the corner that serves as my toilet. None of the children venture down to this end of the hallway. Neither do my parents. I guess no one's allowed.

Is this what it feels like to be in solitary confinement?

If I knew that soon I would be out of here and on my way to your house, Sesame, that would make a difference. If I had something to eat, that would make a difference. If I weren't sick and starving and cold, that would make a difference.

You want to know what happened to the pencil after Deeson clawed it out of the crawl space and handed it to

156

the prft? He put it on display. It's in the Room of Secular Refuse, propped up on the display table. What else is on the Secular Refuse table: that same condom (still in its wrapper). Andrea K's debit card. A bottle of beer. A pink hairbrush (plastic). And now my pencil, with the impression of Deeson's shitty claw fingers imprinted on it in crawlspace dust. How I know this is because they unlocked the laundry room and marched me out and down the hall and through the big door and down the other hallway to show it to me.

My big outing.

Like seeing my pencil was going to impress upon me the seriousness of my crimes? I haven't even done anything. Hear that, assholes? *I didn't do anything.*

I won't call it a compound.

I won't call him the Prophet.

I won't call my pencil Refuse from the Secular World.

Makes me sick to have the prft or Deeson's DNA on anything that's mine, but whatever. We're all breathing in each other's DNA down here. And up there, up in the real world, if you think about it. None of us are immune. Arm yourself with that knowledge, Sesame. Know that it can happen fast. Others have been dragged down slowly, over time, like frogs who start out in cold water over a low flame and end up boiled alive. Be on the lookout.

Sesame

"HI, OFFICER EMMANUEL. It's Sesame Gray."

"Hi, Sesame. How are you?"

"Not good."

"I take it you haven't heard from him yet? That must be very hard, especially on Christmas Eve."

Her voice is polite and gentle, as always. I can sense over the phone that she's just being patient with me. Hearing me out. Probably thinking something like, *The poor girl doesn't want to believe that her boyfriend's breaking up with her/ghosting her/doesn't want to be with her anymore/decided that an extended camping trip with his brainwashed mother and father is preferable to being with her.* Those thoughts come crowding into my brain, but I push them away. I will keep Micah on Officer Emmanuel's radar if it means I have to call every. Single. Day.

After hanging up, I head outside. Into the breach, as someone once said in a poem, or a play, or a novel that I read somewhere. Or watched. Or listened to. I don't know. Lines from poems are blurring around in my head. It's hard to think when Micah's been gone so long. When I haven't heard anything from him. When every day my goal to find him brings nothing.

The stack of notes and poems from the poem boxes grows daily. People are taking the flyers, but no one's called with a possible sighting. A week ago the notes were short and full of energy:

I hope you find him!

I'll be on the lookout!

HE'S CUTE! I'M SORRY HE'S MISSING!

Lots of exclamation points. Lots of smiley faces. Lots of sad faces. As the days have gone by, though, the notes have become more elaborate. There's always at least one new one in each poem box. I make my rounds every day, restocking the boxes with Micah flyers and removing the notes people have left behind.

Dear poem box attendant, my family and I don't know who you are but we enjoy reading the poems you leave. The poem box is a great addition to the neighborhood. PS. We are on the lookout for Micah Stone.

Dear friend of Micah, just FYI we put one of these flyers on our fridge to remind ourselves every day to look for Micah. We have trained ourselves to scan every face on the bus and light rail. Even just crossing the street downtown, we are looking for him.

Dear poem person, Come back, Micah. Micah, come back. Come back, Micah. Micah, come back. This is what I say to myself every morning and night. It's like a prayer but I am not religious. Call it a chant. Know that you are not alone looking for him.

It's hard not to feel alone, searching for Micah, but the notes help. I have no idea who any of these people are, and I guess they have no idea who I am, but we all love poetry. And even though I'm the only one of us who actually knows and loves Micah, it still helps, even a tiny bit, to know that others are thinking about him.

Prince and Peabop are dogs but they *do* know Micah and

they *do* love him. Every morning, before our first search-and-rescue walk of the day, I kneel down in front of them and explain what we are about to do. I recap the whole situation: the Prophet, Micah's worry about his parents, the South Compound. I remind them that this is a search-and-*rescue* mission, not a search-and-*recovery* mission. Big difference. Huge difference.

"So that's the deal," I say, every day, and every day I hold out one of Micah's T-shirts from his dirty laundry basket for them to sniff. "Take a good whiff. We're going to find him, and I can't do it without your help."

I swear to God they understand me. They look at me, look at the T-shirt, snuff its scent up into their dog noses, and sit back on their hind legs, ready for the leash. Then we ease out the Jameses' front door into the city to search. As we walk up and down the streets and alleys, I tell them they need to be careful if they ever run into a dog like the Prophet, a dog who will drag them down into the darkness with him. I've started talking out loud to the pups, telling them they need to be vigilant and protect themselves.

"Here's the thing, though," I tell them. "Ask for help. Definitely ask for help, from the Jameses, from other dogs. Don't be afraid to ask for help."

People sometimes look at me a little funny when they hear me talking to the pups, but I don't care. The pups and I are on a mission and they're not. Something else I've started doing, besides poking my stick into vents and cracks, and calling through broken windows, is looking for footprints in the unplowed lots next to them. It hasn't snowed since Micah disappeared, and footprints leading to the door of an abandoned building would be a definite clue.

(1) A white passenger van with a GOT HOCKEY? bumper sticker, along with (2) footprints leading from it to the door of an abandoned building, along with (3) a sound of any kind in answer to my calling, "Micah! Micah? Are you in there?" when I run my stick into broken windows and vents?

That would be the trifecta of the Micah Stone search-and-rescue mission.

"Micah! MICAH!" I call now. We are at the back door of a half-demolished building. It doesn't fit the exact definition of an abandoned building, but so what. "Anybody here?"

I also keep a lookout for bushes and hedges that might be hiding secret doors. Any place where someone could lie in wait for another human being and then pop out and drag them underground. You can drag people underground in broad daylight, though. All you have to do is change their brains. Tweak the way they think, little by little by little, until you wake up one day and realize the tipping point was reached while you were standing by, ignorant, thinking everything would be okay. And now they're missing.

Nighttime is the hardest. When the sun is out, even if it's behind clouds, I feel stronger. I go through step one and step two and step three as many times as I need to, and I keep moving, because it's daytime and I've got Prince and Peabop, and the world is awake. But at night, ugh. The city and the alley and the walls of my house close down and close in. Nighttime is when the panic flame jumps up, like someone put a match to dry kindling that's been waiting all day long to burst into fire.

And the worst thing? I can't do anything. I can't go out in the dark cold with a flashlight and look for him all night long. But not looking for him feels like a crime. Like I'm letting him down, like I'm wasting precious time, like every minute I'm not searching for him is a minute wasted, but the fact is I have to sleep or I won't be able to search when it's light again. The Jameses are sleeping, Prince and Peabop are sleeping, Inky and Sebastian are sleeping.

Micah, wherever you are, are you sleeping?

Micah, I hate that I'm in my house sitting on my bed not doing anything. I get into bed and I pull the quilts up and I stare up at the skylight and every time I start to get sleepy it feels as if I'm betraying you.

Step one: Don't panic. Panic will accomplish nothing. You can figure this out.

I decide to switch my thoughts away from the fact that the more time passes, the more dangerous it is for him. I decide to imagine that he's here next to me and we're talking, but that instantly reminds me that he's *not* here and we're *not* talking. It hurts too much.

My grandmother used to ask me a question about hurt.

"Are you hurting either yourself or the world, Sesame?" If the answers were No and No, then . . . fine. Go ahead. That was why she would have been all right with me transferring out of regular high school and into New World Online Academy: I was not hurting myself—she knew I hated being on anyone else's schedule—and I was not hurting the world. I mean, did the world care if I finished high school online? No.

In the wake of her dying, I sometimes pretend I'm her. I ask myself the questions that she used to ask me. *Are you hurting either yourself or the world, Sesame?* If the answers are No and No, then . . . okay. *You may proceed, Sesame.*

But, Grandma, here's the thing. Maybe it's bigger than that. Saying No and No to everything starts to feel small and sad. What about Yes and Yes?

Are you being good to yourself, Sesame? Are you being good to the world, Sesame?

Maybe those are better questions.

It hurts way too much to think about my grandmother and Micah.

I decide to think instead about the paper I have to write for school. I'm already past the deadline, but the teacher said I can turn it in anytime over winter break. School is neutral. Homework is neutral. At New World Online Academy, all subjects flow into each other. Whatever you choose to study, you and your teachers figure out how words and art and math and history and science and movement—which is the term they use instead of phys ed—are included on an essential level. "Essential level" is another of their terms. New World was designed for working adults who have not graduated from high school but who want to. Who want to very much.

Question: *But couldn't you just get your GED if you don't want to go to regular school?* That was Inky and Sebastian, when I told them I was sick of normal high school, that I was going to finish high school at New World, after I explained how it worked.

Answer: *Yes.* But I wanted more than my GED, and so does everyone else enrolled at New World. A high school diploma from New World Online Academy is a door opening onto the future, and a GED is a door closing on the past. They're both good, but they're good in different ways.

Everyone works alone at New World, but we all know of each other's existence. We all know that we are out here in the city, roaming the streets, working at our jobs and school at the same time. We meet up in our online classes, which are held at unusual times, like 5–7 a.m., or 11–1 a.m. p.m., or 4–6 p.m., or 9–11 p.m. Times when the rest of the world can possibly do without a working adult, or a second parent. Times when a determined person can squeeze in a couple of hours to focus on a teacher, to take notes, to ask questions. And then figure out how to construct and complete a project that "will reflect and synthesize what you have learned in a way that is personally meaningful and socially significant."

We all have avatars. They're animated. C. Lee's is a rainbow unicorn. D. Mobry's is a feral pig. J. Abebe's is a dancing apple pie. S. Potter's is Princess Leia. Mine is Goth Hello Kitty. I chose Goth Kitty in honor of the notebook that Vong gave to Micah.

One year left to go at New World.

My paper's topic: "The Personal Impact of Anonymous Poems Given as Gifts."

You can do all your homework for New World on your phone. That's how I do it, anyway. Research, document, write your papers, send them in, check for your grade. Simple. Sometimes I wake up in the middle of the night, and if I can't get back to sleep, I work on my papers in the dark. Me and my glowing electric fireplace and the skylight glowing down on my glowing phone, where my fingers are picking out the words one letter at a time, like right now.

I flip from my paper to my messages to make sure nothing randomly popped in without notifying me. Nothing. I check again. And again. And again, because I'm a robot who can't stop checking. This is what panic does. *Stop, Sesame.*

I open up my photos instead. Swipe and swipe and swipe and swipe.

See this photo of my grandmother? Can you tell what she's holding? It's kind of shadowy, I know. A plateful of dumplings, that's what. That black spot is the little bowl of dipping sauce.

See this one of Inky? It's before she cut her hair. Her hair was crazy. I loved it but she didn't.

See this one of Sebastian? Look at his feet. He's hiding behind the table, but you can still see his hairy toe poking out. Loud and proud, men who wear Birkies.

See this other one of my grandmother? She just got home from work. Still wearing that white apron. She didn't bother to take it off, usually. So when I think of my grandmother, she pops into my head wearing a white apron.

See this one of Inky and Sebastian in the conference room? They're sitting straight up like that and not smiling, because they wanted to look like members of the board. That's also why they're each holding a pen in their hand, and also why Sebastian's feet are tucked behind his chair. Members of the board don't wear Birkies. At least we don't think they do. None of us really know what a member of the board is, or does. Or what it even means to be a member of a board.

See this one? Tell me which one is Prince. That's right, the one with the purple bandanna. We're standing on the western shore of Lake of the Isles. That thing in the background is Minne, the Minneapolis lake monster. She appears in the spring and makes her way from lake to lake. I tried to get those pups to look menacing, but it's not in their nature. At the last second Peabop put her paw on top of Prince's. I know. It almost makes me cry to look at it. She loves him.

See these two guys? Tell me who they are. Correct. James One is on the left and James Two is on the right. Neither dog is in the photo because I wanted a photo of just the Jameses. This was taken after I had just started working for them. The reason they look serious, which they almost never do, is because they had found out my grandmother had died. They wouldn't have found out except that James Two handed me my check, and suddenly I thought, *She'll never see this check*, and for some reason I started crying. I mean, who cares if your grandmother sees your check, right?

See this? It's dark, because it's often kind of dark in my house, but can you tell what it is? That's right, it's the recliner that my former neighbors Brian and Chee gave me before they moved to China. You can't tell from the photo, but it's dark red, like a wine-red leather, and soft and smooth. Peabop and Prince would love that recliner. So would James One and James Two, come to think of it.

See this? Guess what it's a photo of. No. It is not an abandoned garage. But I'm glad you think it's one, because that's what I want you to think. This is my house.

See this one? It's a screenshot of Goth Hello Kitty, my avatar at New World Online Academy.

This one? It's me and Micah in my house late at night. Look close and you can see a slightly less-black squarish thing. That's the skylight. This photo was taken last fall, during the first snowfall. We were lying on the bed next to the fireplace, looking up. First one snowflake, then another, then so many that the sky was blotted out and so was the skylight. No one but me and Micah would ever know what this is a photo of.

This one is Micah hiding behind the R in LIBRARY behind the Walker Library. It was August and we had just come from the Minneapolis Sculpture Garden, where Micah hid behind the spoon of the Spoonbridge and Cherry sculpture. We walked back to Uptown from there. Along the way Micah hid behind things—the bus stop shelter, the concrete wall by the Y, the brick pillar by the Uptown Theatre—and I took photos of Micah hiding. No one looking at these photos would know that Micah was in them, but Micah and I do.

We stopped at Kowalski's because Sebastian was Employee of the Month, and then we stopped at Spyhouse Coffee because Inky was working.

This one is a photo of Sebastian at Kowalski's, posing on the stairs by his Employee of the Month photo. No one but the three of us—Sebastian, Micah, and me—know that Micah was standing sideways behind Sebastian and that Sebastian's body entirely hid Micah's.

This one is a photo of Inky standing in front of the counter at Spyhouse Coffee with her arms spread wide, singing "Ave Maria." No one but me and Micah would know he was actually hiding behind the counter.

This one is a photo of Micah walking backward down Hennepin ahead of me, holding his ice cream cone behind his back. No one but me and Micah would know he had one in his hand.

This one is a photo of Micah standing in front of the huge lilac bush a few yards away from the bus stop at 34th and Hennepin. No one but me would know that he was about to kiss me, and then kiss me again, and then decide that he didn't need to go home yet, and then walk to my house holding my hand, and wait until I slipped around the side of my house and went in first, and then he followed, and shut the door.

The thing about photos is they're as much about what you can't see and don't know as what you do.

15

Micah

WHEN MY PARENTS took down the artwork and photos, I should've called them on it. When they whitewashed all the walls, I should've called them on it. When they quit their jobs, I should've called them on it. When they laid their phones down on the counter without a word of protest and followed Deeson out into the freezing night, I should've run like hell.

When you don't and don't and don't call anyone out on their shit, shit just keeps happening.

And you end up somewhere, you don't know where, belowground and cold and hungry and almost out of points and wondering how the fuck you got there.

How everything went to shit. Every daynight, which is how I think of time now, points are being deducted.

> Deeson: "That'll be another five points, Stone."

Me: "Why?"

> Deeson: "Infraction."

Me: "For what?"

> Deeson: "Insubordination."

Me: "What happens again when all the points are gone? I get cast out of eden, right? Something like that?"

> Deeson smiles. Says nothing.

A Deeson smile without an answer is another sign, a sign of nothing good. The box is closing in. The points are evaporating and so is my body. You used to say I was skinny for a guy whose native language is Food, Sesame, but *this* is what skinny looks like. This right here. Ribs and joints that poke out, that are countable, that skin is stretched tight across. The cement floor is cold, the cement walls are cold, the dripping white robes drip cold, and cold has settled into me.

Sometimes I think, *What if I die down here?*

They only unlock the door now to announce a new infraction in front of everyone. Deeson and the prft herd me to the Room of Reflection. All the Lights are there, in their white robes that I have washed for them, and they all hold hands. *Bless the child, bless the child, bless the child.* Maybe they're starting to forget all the words they used to know.

"Hey, I washed that robe," I say as Deeson and the prft march me past everyone. "I washed your robe, and your robe, and your robe, and your robe, and your robe, and . . ."

Except that's a lie. I don't say anything. I don't even look at anyone. And no one but the prft and Deeson and my parents look at me. There's a weird look in my parents' eyes when they look at me. It's like I'm becoming a ghost to them. Like they've given up on me.

Sesame, I don't know where I am. I'm getting confused. It's daynight and it's cold and Deeson and the prft hate me.

Sesame, I'm working on a theory—that life is like a series of concentric boxes. There's the box you live in with your parents, and it has its own rules and rituals, and they're in charge. Then there's the box that surrounds that box, and it's made of school and the city you live in and the government, and they're all in charge. Then there's the bigger, invisible box that surrounds the other boxes, and it's made up of what you believe plus how people perceive you. That one's a powerful box. It can be made of religion.

Or megalomania, in which someone has delusional fantasies of wealth, power, and omnipotence. If this box surrounds you, it's hard not to succumb.

The box of megalomania has to be counteracted with another box, Sesame. I need another box. A bigger box. A more powerful box.

Am I making sense?

Hello Kitty is still hidden in the crawl space behind the vent.

So is the potato.

I will not eat the potato.

If I eat the potato, that will be a sign I have given up.

Because if I eat the potato, the potato will cease life.

All the potatoes it could have produced will be lost along with it.

It's like the future would no longer exist.

I will not eat the potato.

I'm waiting for a sign.

Things are bad.

How to Cope

Don't panic. Distract yourself from panic. Panic won't solve anything. Think of you instead.

Me: Who's your favorite poet, Sesame?

You closed your eyes and shook your head. You hate this question. Too many poets, too little time.

Me: You want to go re-poem tonight?

You nodded. Yes to re-poeming. Remember the night

we went re-poeming in the first snow? Each of us with pockets full of scrolled-up poems printed out on pink and yellow and green and blue paper. Easter egg colors in November. The streets are magical in first snow. Our footprints made dark tracks behind us, the snow was that light and soft and new. No wind. No gloves, no jackets. We untacked a blanket from the wall and wrapped it around both of us, and up and down the alleys we went.

We were alley people. You taught me that, Sesame.

"There are sidewalk people and there are alley people," you said.

"And we are of the alley," I said.

We hunched down underneath our blanket and prowled the alleys like cat people. We were the cat people of the alleys. We were the poem people of South Minneapolis. Catch us if you can.

"It's hard to be a cat-poem person of the alleys when you have to share a single blanket with another cat-poem person," I said.

"Hard, yes," you said. "Hard for sure. But not impossible."

Sesame, do you remember which blanket we had with us that night?

I can't remember. I'm getting confused.

Remember how the first day in the alley between Bryant and Colfax you stood there all suspicious? Keeping tight hold of the leash even though it was clear the dogs weren't afraid of me? It was just us in the alley. No cars.

No one walking out from their backyard to their garage. I remember that the Lunds bag in my arms didn't feel light or heavy. In fact, I had forgotten I was holding it.

"What's in the bag?" you asked me.

"Potatoes," I said.

"I like potatoes," you said. "Mashed are my favorite."

That changed things somehow. You changed from a suspicious girl into a girl who liked mashed potatoes. You looked familiar suddenly, like you were a girl I knew, or should know. You stood there with the dogs and the leash and something in your hands. Later I knew they were poems, and that you were on your re-poeming rounds, but I didn't know that then. Prince lay down at that point, he was that unconcerned. Then I realized that I did know you. You used to go to Lake Harriet. You used to sit on the far side of the room from me, next to the window that Ms. Adebayo kept cracked open year-round. Fall winter spring, you sat next to that window and I sat next to the door. Opposite sides of the room, except maybe it meant the same thing: we both needed to be near an exit. An escape. A way out.

You shifted a little, then. You lifted a shoulder. You were standing there so still. I wanted to keep talking to you, continue the potato conversation.

"Mashed are good," I said. "Baked are good. So are fried. It's hard to ruin a potato."

You stood very still. But you smiled. I wanted you to

keep looking at me and talking to me. I wanted to keep hearing your voice. If I could hear your voice again. That's what I remember thinking, or feeling: *If I can keep hearing her voice.*

I try not to challenge him, but it happens. It happens over and over. Because words, Ses. Words matter. Conjugate is not the same as contemplate. If I used the word "conjugate" and you knew I meant "contemplate," and you said, *You mean "contemplate"?* I'd be happy. Grateful. Thank you, Ses, for correcting me.

Not so with the prft. He's not correctable. Any correction or suggestion or hint that he's not perfect, and his entire sense of identity is threatened. Look at him, poor guy who has to believe that he's a god among men. Poor guy who has to think that he and he alone knows the truth. Poor guy who has to be surrounded with a crowd of adoring sycophants—know that word, prft? I'm guessing not— or the world will fall apart.

It'd be sad. If it weren't so fucking dangerous.

I've had a lot of time to conjugate my future, and it looks like this:

> (A) I'm alive and underground
> (B) I'm dead and underground
> (C) I'm alive and aboveground
> (D) I'm dead and aboveground

Those are the four conjugations of Micah. I've come to believe that dead is a distinct possibility. That's not an overstatement. If he could get rid of the thorn in his side, the single unbeliever in the midst of his fearful throng, he'd do it and he wouldn't think twice. I don't believe in an afterlife and I don't believe in the prft, but I believe that the prft would kill me in a heartbeat if he could get away with it. Have me killed. Would have me killed. Will have me killed. See? I can conjugate. I'm really good at conjugating.

I'm not so good at laundry.

I used to be—I think, anyway—but it's hard to wash so many clothes. Hard to get them clean, hard to rinse them. Hard to hoist them over the clotheslines. They weigh so much. And I'm so tired. I'm so weak. There's so much water. It drips down, it trickles down. Then they tell me the robes are still dirty, still damp, and they haul me out and down to the Room of Reflection in front of everyone. Infraction. Infractions cost points.

My hands are cracked and bleeding. Sometimes I put my fingers in my mouth to keep them warm and stop them from bleeding, even for a few minutes.

How would he do it? Deeson, probably. The prft wouldn't want to get his hands dirty in the actual doing of the deed. He's shut me down as much as he can: banishment to the laundry room, confiscation of pencil, decree of non-verbality unless he's asking me a direct question. Forced fasting. Which is something I haven't told you about, Sesame. Or wait, have I? Starvation. Nothing's worked so far. I mean, starvation's working, but maybe it's too slow for them. Time to bring in the big guns, which here in the belowground means Deeson. He's the only one with the balls to do it. Whatever the prft decrees, Deeson's on it. Would be on it. Would have been on it. Will be on it. See what I did there? Conjugation. It's a useful tool.

It's dark down here. Maybe he'll wait until everyone else is sleeping, then sneak into the laundry room, find me in the corner, and press a pillow over my face until I'm dead. Maybe he'll strangle me with his belt. Maybe he'll stab me with a kitchen knife.

There's any number of ways to kill a person.

Maybe, once my lifeless body is found, Deeson will get a reward. Maybe the prft will let him wear the headlamp for an hour a day. Maybe he'll get extra prayers. Maybe he'll get extra rations. That's what the prft calls them now: rations.

And everyone just goes along with it. The prft calls food "rations," so everyone else does too. The prft decrees that only bare overhead bulbs are allowed, no one complains. The prft glares his headlamp into the face of anyone he looks at now—not just me anymore—and no one does anything but blink and squint and try not to flinch.

Why? Because no one will call him out.

Why not? Because everyone is afraid.

What are they afraid of? The rage of the prft.

So everyone walks on eggshells. It's a minefield of

broken eggs down here, Sesame. What's it like up there? Has winter turned to spring yet? How are Prince and Peabop? How are the Jameses? Are you reading in the recliner? Are the poem boxes full of poems? Has anyone found your house? Has anyone figured you out? Is it day or night out right now? I send you these thoughts from a place where the days are growing shorter. The light is dwindling, Sesame.

16

Sesame

INKY AND SEBASTIAN and I meet in the conference room, because the library is open again after being closed for Christmas Day. It's not even decorated, nor was it ever, maybe because of freedom from religion? This is a relief, because Christmas trees and Christmas lights and Christmas music have been everywhere else I go, and all the happiness and excitement just make Micah's absence worse.

I didn't want to put up a tiny tree in my house, even though I usually do in honor of my grandmother, but I didn't *not* want to either. It felt wrong to decorate for Christmas with Micah gone—like, there should be no celebrations until he's back—but it also felt wrong not to.

I mean, I do have a present for him. The stack of notes and poems on the table gets bigger every day. I compromised by draping a string of twinkle lights around the poems table and Micah's present.

Inky and Sebastian both come from big Christmas-celebrating families. They each invited me to their house for the day yesterday, but I said no. Precious daylight hours needed to be spent searching, even on Christmas.

"Ses, I thought of something," Inky says now. "Have you checked his OverDrive library account? Because maybe he's—" I shake my head. Yes, I checked, the day after he disappeared and every day since. Nothing.

"Fuck."

She's pissed. Not at me, not at Micah, but at the fact that the one barely possible explanation anyone's had—that somehow Micah's parents *did* just up and haul him on a camping trip, and he's somehow borrowing library books on his audio account—was so quickly shot down.

"I put up more flyers," I say, ticking things off on my fingers. "The white passenger van count is up to twelve, but none are cult vans. The abandoned building count is up to fifteen, but they all seem truly abandoned. I call Officer Emmanuel daily just to stay on her radar. The Jameses take turns calling all the hospitals. Prince and Peabop and I have tripled our walks."

The Jameses are okay with this. The dogs and I go out early. After an hour we're too cold, so I take them into a dog-friendly place until we're warm again and then back out we go for another hour. We repeat this one more time before the sun goes down, which it does around four forty-five, and that's it for the day.

"How do you know they're searching?" Sebastian says. "Do they look any different from the way they do on a regular walk?"

"Yes," I say. "They're more businesslike."

Inky sucks in a deep breath and frowns, and I tense.

"Ses," she says, then hesitates. Looks at Sebastian. They're communicating something to each other.

"What?" I say. "Spit it out."

"Ses," Inky says again, "I'm sorry, but Sebastian and I have to bring something up again. Which is, could the Stones actually be where they say they are? Down south on a tech-free camping trip? Is that *at all* a possibility?"

She's talking fast, her eyes down. When she's done, she glances up, a look of fear in her eyes. Is Inky afraid of me? Afraid of what I'll say?

"What the hell, Inky," I say, and I look over at Sebastian. He's got the same look on his face. Have they been talking about me? Wondering if I've lost it? If I actually made this whole thing up? I imagine it, the two of them texting while I'm out walking the dogs and searching. Late-night conversations when they're both off work and at home. Speculating that maybe the Stones are for real, that the note they sent to school is legit, that the reason the police aren't paying any attention to my missing person report is because Micah's not actually missing.

"No," I say. "It's not a possibility."

"Okay," Sebastian says hastily, and "All right," Inky says. They're acting like they don't want to make me angry. Like they're scared of me. Can that be right?

"What's going on here?" I say. "Are you two scared of me?"

Sebastian clears his throat. "Not scared *of* you," he says. "Maybe scared a little bit *for* you."

"We're not as sure of the situation as you are," Inky says carefully, like she's clarifying. "When you look at it objectively, it does seem possible that everything in the note Mr. and Mrs. Stone sent to Southwest is actually true. Like maybe they *are* just on a tech-free camping trip."

I say nothing. My heart is pounding. Inky and Sebastian are my best friends. And my best friends don't believe me. Or they're starting not to believe me. Sebastian picks up where Inky leaves off.

"Plus, Ses, the police see hundreds of missing person reports every month, right?" he says. "They have experience with this kind of thing. And they're not even a little bit concerned."

I still haven't said anything. Neither of them can tell that my heart is racing and I feel like puking—they don't believe me! They don't think Micah's in danger!—and then Inky says something that hits me right in the gut.

"Ses, I hate to say this, but when you look at the bigger picture, you're pretty mysterious yourself."

Sebastian nods—they *have* been talking about me—and

starts talking. "Number one, Inky and I have never even met your aunt. We barely even met your grandmother! Number two, your aunt's *still* in California taking care of a sick friend?"

"Which, number three, means you're totally alone right now," Inky says. "And you were alone on Christmas."

"But you wouldn't come over to either of our houses," Sebastian says. "That's just . . . awful."

"And weird," Inky says. "And the last thing? We don't even know where you live. That's not right."

They're piling on and I feel dizzy. It's hard to breathe. My two best friends are looking at me with suspicion, and I suddenly want my grandmother so bad I can't breathe. Can't think. No, what I want is Micah. Micah knows everything about me. When I'm with Micah, I'm not hiding anything. I pick up my backpack and sling it over my shoulders. Inky jumps up and comes around to me.

"Ses, please don't go. We're *worried* about you."

"I don't have time for this shit," I say, and I blow out of the conference room. Our conference room.

It's hard to breathe, hard to think—they're my *best friends*—but I keep moving. I go straight to the Jameses and pick up the dogs. Out we go, tromping the alleys with the staple gun and extra flyers. I restaple flyers that are coming loose, put up new ones, load up the poem boxes with Micah's smiling face. More notes have appeared.

I'm sorry about your friend. This is a hard time of year to be missing someone.

We will be on the lookout. I lit a
candle for him last night.

*Thank you for the poems and sorry about
your missing friend. I would say Merry
Christmas but that doesn't seem right, so I
will just say keep the faith.*

HAVE NOT SEEN THIS BOY BUT I'M KEEPING MY
EYES OPEN.

These note-writing strangers are kinder than Sebastian
and Inky. *That's not true, Sesame.* It feels true right now,
though. What's worse is knowing that they doubt he's
in danger. *Is* he in danger, Sesame? Yes. He's in danger,
because if Micah wasn't in danger, he'd be with me. That
is 100 percent clear. It's been fourteen days now, and fourteen days is a long time. Stapling up flyers and leaving them
in the poem boxes feels like a stupid thing to do in the face
of . . .

What if he never comes back?

No, don't think like that. Don't even let that thought
into your brain. Then they've won.

Three little phones lined up by the toaster.

I'm trying not to panic.

*Think of something good, Sesame. Think of a good person.
Good people.* People like Brian and Chee, my former neighbors who moved to China last summer. They used to live

down the block in the six-plex. One day I was walking
home down the alley and it was like an entire apartment
had been dragged out to the garbage: a dining table, a desk
and chair, a laundry drying rack, a bookcase with all the
books still in it, a small Persian rug, and the recliner. It's
real leather, dyed dark red. I sat right down in it. Everything was set up like it was a living room, right out there
in the sunshine, late on a Tuesday afternoon. I leaned back
and popped out the recliner footrest and closed my eyes,
like I was some business executive from the 1950s, home
from another cutthroat day and ready for a drink.

"You want that recliner? You can have it."

I opened my eyes. Two guys were standing by the garbage cans, looking at me. They looked happy to see me
sitting in their recliner, as though they had needed a girl
to complete their domestic scene and suddenly, there I
was.

"We're moving," the tall guy said. "Like, tomorrow."

"To China," the short guy said. "So we have to get
rid of all our stuff. We got married last week and we're
moving to Beijing tomorrow," he added, and the tall guy
put his arm around the other guy's shoulder and beamed.
That's the only word for it. The sunlight of their happiness
glowed out from them and fell on me, and I wanted to ask
them if I could move to China with them, because then
the warmth of their happiness would spill onto me and I
would be happy too. That's how it felt, being in their presence. That's the kind of person you have to think of when

you're trying to keep going. The kind of people who give off warmth.

"I'd love this recliner," I said.

"It's custom-dyed," the tall one said, and he held out his hand to me. "I'm Chee."

"I'm Brian," the short one said. "Where do you live? Can we help you move it?"

They were the nicest guys. In my memory, they will always be the nicest guys in the world. Brian and Chee. Where are they now? I sometimes wonder. Late at night, when I'm reading in my custom-dyed dark red recliner, I wonder. I hope they're still in China, eating noodle soup and dumplings, speaking Chinese, holding hands and laughing.

"I'll get my boyfriend to help me later," I said. "He's got a truck."

They looked at each other and nodded approvingly, like, of course this girl has a boyfriend with a truck. They liked me instantly and vice versa. It was one of those things.

"I wish you weren't moving to China," I said, and they made faces and tilted their heads and kept nodding, like, *We wish we weren't moving to China either, now that we just met you and it's the start of a beautiful friendship.*

That was the last time I saw Brian and Chee. Late that night, when the city was dark and quiet, I snuck up the alley and spread a big piece of plastic in front of the recliner where Brian and Chee had dragged it behind the garage so no one else would take it. They had covered it with the rug because I wanted that, too. Then I tipped the recliner onto the plastic—it was thick and heavy plastic, the kind professional painters use—and I dragged the whole thing down the alley.

I'm thinking about the recliner now, as I try *not* to think about Sebastian and Inky. As I staple up flyers and collect notes and poems for Micah and scan the alleys and curbs for white vans and abandoned buildings and footprints across pristine snowy parking lots.

That recliner was heavy. It was the kind of thing that most people wouldn't think of moving alone. It was hard to move and it took a while. But you know what? I made it.

Screw you, everyone who doesn't believe that Micah's in trouble.

Onward.

17

Micah

MY PARENTS ARE shorn. Deeson cut their hair. He's cut everyone's hair except his own and the prft's. And mine. They must be saving me for something special.

I didn't see Deeson cut my parents' hair, but I wish I had. Because then I wouldn't have these mind images to contend with. Like my mom with the tarp draped over her, the scissors in Deeson's hands. All her long brown hair drifting in clouds to the floor. And then the razor. Her eyes, blinking like a baby bird's. Her head like a chemo patient's head but no scarf and no hat to keep her skull warm. Deeson and his smirk.

Deeson told me they're talking about a purification

ceremony for me now. The prft wants a ritual cleansing. Back in the day, the word "cleanse" meant to clean. To get the dirt out. It must have been a good word back then, untainted and straightforward. Now it's a dark word. Stained. Like think about what the phrase ethnic cleansing really means.

The laundry room smells. Like laundry, and detergent, and dampness, and also like a toilet, because it is. They don't let me out anymore, so I can't empty my toilet bucket.

The last time they did let me out was to see their new ritual: duct-taping the items on the Refuse from the Secular World table. Around and around and around my pencil the prft wound the roll of tape, while Deeson the acolyte held it steady. Deeson who stands at the right hand of the prft, ready to carry out his every bidding. Then they laid the duct-taped pencil down in state on the table, along with the condom and the pink hairbrush and a grocery list and the debit card, all of which they also duct-taped. So they're unrecognizable, I guess.

Sesame. Sesame. Can you hear me rambling on and on and on? Are any of my thoughts getting through to you?

Sesame, it's harder than I thought it would be, down here. I don't see my parents much. Lie. I don't see my parents ever anymore. *Wheresoever the sin was committed, there shall the sinner reside.* Did my parents commit a sin? Are they residing where their sin was committed? I don't know. The daynights have all run together, and when was the last time I actually talked to them? Deeson the anointed was the bearer of the sin news, announced that during prayers after the ritual duct-taping of the pencil. He stood next to the prft and he read from a card that the prft handed him. He had to hold it as far away from himself as he could, the way that middle-aged people do. Guy must be too vain to wear reading glasses. Unless reading glasses are also forbidden. Part of the refuse from the secular world.

Maybe it's good I can't see my parents. I used to feel sad and worried for them, but I don't anymore. Now all I feel is angry. Aren't they supposed to take care of me and not the other way around? How did everything get so messed up?

All my points are gone. The prft and Deeson are talking about the Court of Ascendance Law. They're talking about eden and being cast out of it. I don't know what that means. What happens now is beyond my control and probably beyond my parents' control, even though my parents are so much older than me. They've lived through a lot more years than me and a lot of things that I don't even know about because I wasn't born yet. Did they have a defining moment somewhere along the way that made them strangely susceptible to the prft? In some ways, I hope so. Because if the answer is no, then it means that what happened to them could happen to anyone.

≻ ≻ ≻

In my corner of the laundry room I'm looking through a mental telescope at human history, and what I'm seeing is some human beings trying to hold back other humans every step of the way. There's no end to it. It happens everywhere. Everywhere in the world are cement-block laundry rooms, and in the corner of every one of them is a huddled-up human wondering where the light went.

Be vigilant, my child. Protect yourself.

Ses, you told me that's what your grandmother always told you. I'm sorry, Ses. I wish I had been more vigilant. I wish I had protected myself. Maybe then this laundry room and my parents' bald skulls and my duct-taped pencil would never have happened.

Sesame, please be out there fighting. Please be filling the boxes with poems. Please be surrounded with Peabop and Prince and Inky and Sebastian and the Jameses.

Remember when you told me your favorite food was pot stickers, how your grandmother made them for you every weekend, how she told you to crimp the hell out of them, how she cheated and used angel hair coleslaw instead of chopping the cabbage by hand, how she made you as many as you wanted and there were always, always, always enough?

In our nameless café, there will always be enough food.

In the world I want to live in, there will always be enough everything.

This is me talking to you, Sesame. This is my internal,

no-spoken-or-written-words account of what it was like to descend into the underground and then, bit by bit and day by day, have your life taken away from you. Don't let your life be taken away from you, Sesame. Wherever you are in this daynight world, know this: if I don't make it out of here, you were my enough.

18

Sesame

THE WEEK AFTER Christmas I'm usually happy and relieved, because I don't feel left out and alone anymore. And even though I know that not everyone celebrates Christmas, it *feels* as if everyone does. All the trees and lights and carols and red and green. It's overwhelming. It's a relief to have it done.

Except not this year. I keep the pile of notes for Micah from the poem boxes on the table in the corner of my house, and it grows higher every day. I try to tell myself that this is good, because when we find him, he'll be able to read through them all and see how people who don't even know him were rooting for him, which is a good thing. What's not a good thing? That every time I open a poem box and see another note for him, it means we haven't found him.

Officer Emmanuel didn't return my call yesterday. Maybe she's on vacation; maybe she's home with her family. If she has a family. Which she probably does. Because everyone has a family except me. *Stop feeling sorry for yourself, Sesame.*

It has been sixteen days.

Peabop and Prince and I are out walking from alley to alley in a widening square near Southwest High School, which is closed up for winter break, and they keep turning their heads back and up to look at me, like, *Are you okay? What's going on?* You can't lie to a dog. Their senses are lie-proof. They know when you're sad and worried and angry and off-kilter. They know that I'm feeling sorry for myself.

I haven't talked to Sebastian or Inky in two days, since they accused me.

They didn't accuse you, Sesame.

They did. They accused me of lying by omission: about my aunt, about living alone, about where I live.

And the thing is, they were right. I did lie to them. I *am* lying to them.

Grandma, what did being afraid mean to you? How do you want me *not* to be afraid? Human beings lie to each other a lot, pretend to be something they're not. Like Micah pretended—*pretends* to be obedient to the Prophet, and I pretend to have an aunt who takes care of me. And the Prophet? He pretends that he alone knows the one true way to live.

"Things change fast, Sesame," Micah said to me a few nights before he disappeared. "Don't they?"

We were lying on my bed, looking up at the skylight and trying to go back in time and figure out when, exactly, the Prophet had planted the potato of doubt in his parents' hearts. Had it happened the very night of Micah's thirteenth birthday party?

"Does he have some kind of actual power?" Micah said. "Or is he just an asshole that people are afraid of so they follow him?"

"Being an asshole that people are afraid of *is* actual power," I said.

"How do you take it away then?"

"You can't push a string," I said. Which is something else my grandmother used to say.

"What does that mean?"

But I didn't have a good answer. I had never really understood it when my grandmother said it. Now, though, I think about it. There are forces in the world that pull people toward each other and push them apart. You can pull a string but you can't push it. So maybe the only way people like the Prophet lose their power is when people stop believing them.

Peabop and Prince and I are the only ones walking the alleys. That's the way it seems, at any rate. Everyone else is warm and safe in their houses and apartments, full of leftover Christmas food, looking through their presents, drinking coffee, lazing around. That's what I imagine, anyway. The pups keep turning their heads inquiringly, like, *What's wrong, Sesame?* I tug at the leash and we keep moving. We stop only when I spot a white van or a building that looks abandoned.

Peer into the van. Does it look recently used? Are there car seats in it, or evidence of non–Living Lightly life? The answer is always yes. So far.

If there's an abandoned parking lot by the abandoned building, scan it for footprints. It's been a long time since it snowed, and it's packed and hard in the cold, but footprints in parking lots are still visible.

Run the stick along the building.

Poke it into the vents.

Crouch down and yell into every vent on every building that looks abandoned.

I'm not careful anymore. I just scream his name. "MICAH! MICAAAAAAH!" What's the harm in yelling? Can't hurt, right?

Back to pretense. The why of the pretense is more important than the pretense. Micah pretended to listen to the Prophet so that he could watch over his parents. I pretend so that I can make my own decisions for myself. So nobody has power over me. The Prophet pretends so that . . . he can have power over others?

There's a lot of pretense in the world, a lot of strutting, a lot of proclamations. A poet said that, I think. My poets are mixing up in my mind, along with potatoes. I mean poems. Are there poems about potatoes? That's a stupid question. My thoughts are disordered. Not enough sleep, too much worry.

Potatoes.

Micah makes sweet potatoes with ginger and butter and sea salt. He roasts them slow. They're going to be on the menu in our nameless café. There's going to be a bookcase full of board games in the corner of our nameless café. There'll be a jar full of dog treats on the top shelf.

Here's an abandoned building, right in the middle of the block. A two-story brick-and-stucco building that looks like an office building, from the back, anyway. I stop before we tromp across the parking lot, and scan it for footprints. Nothing. I run my stick along the foundation, poke it into a cracked window. Most of the windows are boarded up. A broken plastic laundry hamper full of scraps of plastic and metal piping sits next to the locked steel back door. Peabop and Prince sniff at the vents when I call into them, but they want to keep going, so we do.

Micah, are you hungry? Are you cold? Are you exhausted? Are you sick? You have to rally, Micah. You have to send a signal, Micah. You have to help me find you. You have to do your part. You are fading. The scent of you is disappearing on the clothes you left at my house, Micah. I sleep with them because I want to sleep with you, and I breathe in your clothes because I want to smell you next to me, but you are fading out. It's getting bad.

Peabop and Prince turn again and look up at me.

"What is it, you two?" I say.

Their ears prick up. They slow down, and then they stop. We are almost all the way to Espresso of Dreams now, where dogs are welcome and the owners keep a container of dog treats on the counter. But they're not looking at Espresso of Dreams. They're looking at me. Those dark dog eyes, unblinking and calm. Peabop extends her paw. Prince inclines his head. This is how they talk to me. This is one of the ways they talk to me.

"Come on, pups," I say, "we have to find him," and then I start to cry. This is not something I do, ever, except lately. I don't even know *how* to cry, except that apparently I do, because once the tears start splashing out of my eyes, I sink down to a crouch. Peabop and Prince are right there, licking my cheeks and pushing up against me like a dog's version of a hug. I've got my arms around them and I'm heaving with sobs and tears and snot and they just stand still against me, waiting.

Now it's late. Dark. After midnight.

I'm lying in bed, looking up at the skylight, trying not to panic while I wait for morning to come.

I check his OverDrive account for the millionth time. Nothing.

I swipe through our old texts, a nervous habit I have now: up and up and up and down and down and down, scrolling through days and weeks and months of back-

and-forthing between the two of us. I go back in time and relive memories, like that night on the 6 bus when we were heading back to Uptown. We were sitting in the back. Remember, Micah? You put my fare on your Go-To card because you did things like that. You *do* things like that.

We climbed the steps and sat in the back of the bus, in the very last seats. Hardly anyone was on the bus, that late at night, and the late-night-bus sleepy feeling had descended. We were tired from climbing around on the rocks and the trails and running up and down the stairs by the river. The cafés and theater along Saint Anthony Main, by the Mississippi, had gone dark by the time we walked back to the bus stop.

We had known each other for three weeks at that point. We had already started planning for the future. Our trip around the world, and how we could do it as cheap as possible. Where we could learn fire spinning. How maybe we should make a puppet for the May Day parade, and what kind of puppet we should make. The restaurant we ~~were~~ are going to build when we graduate high school. We were already debating possible names for it. But we had not touched each other yet.

Micah, I don't know what you would say to the question *Why not?* but here's my answer: Because it was too big, too important. It meant too much.

There was a wall of want in the air between us. The closer we stood, the thicker it got, and the harder it was to talk around it. Sometimes when you were near me I felt as if the air itself was trembling. Sometimes when I looked up at you that day, when you were ahead of me on the trail, you were looking back at me at the exact same minute, and it was like the air between us changed color.

It was dark and quiet and we were sitting in the way back, you by the window and me in the seat next to you. Each streetlight swept across your hair and your cheeks, and your eyes were dark pools. You weren't looking at me. Sweep of light, darkness. Sweep of light, darkness. Hennepin Avenue rolled by outside the window: the Orpheum Theatre on the right, Minneapolis Community and Technical College on the left. The Sculpture Garden and the Walker. Spyhouse Coffee and Nico's Tacos and then we were closing in on the Uptown YWCA bus transfer station. You weren't looking at me and it was time for me to stand up and walk down the aisle and get off the bus and I reached across you to pull the yellow STOP REQUESTED cord and you turned to me and met my reaching hand with yours. You stopped my hand in midair and held it. And your eyes were those dark pools and I still couldn't see your expression but you were holding my hand and the air, the dark air in the back of the 6 bus, was alive and electric.

You reached up with your other hand and pulled the yellow cord. The bus groaned over to the side of the street. You were still holding my hand.

"Sesame," you said then, or maybe "Safe home" or maybe "I'll see you soon" or maybe "This is just the beginning." Whatever you said, Micah, I carried it with me when you let go of my hand and I turned and walked down the aisle and off the bus into my new life.

19

Micah

I THINK THEY know about the potato. I think they're looking for the potato, and if they find it, that would be reason enough. They would try me in the Court of Ascendance Law, and if the jury finds me guilty, then the prft would sentence me to the punishment he deems fitting. The punishment could be permanent confinement in the laundry room. It could be a several-week fast. It could be a whipping. Any of those sentences could lead to death. Or the sentence could be death itself, carried out by Deeson, who has crossed over into some kind of other country in his mind.

But the potato.

The potato is still hidden behind the vent screen. If I'm careful, no one will find it. I try not to think about or picture the potato because of the chance that my potato will get into the heads of the wrong people. This is always a danger when I'm writing to you in my head, Sesame, but it's doubly dangerous when I think of the potato. If the image of the hidden potato, along with my thoughts about it, get into the heads of the wrong people, then they will know where it is. They will come find it. And when they have the potato, they will also have me.

I don't think I have the strength to deny the potato forcefully enough so that they would believe me. I've dreamed about it, and the dream goes like this:

The door to the laundry room bursts open in the middle of the night. The prft with his headlamp, and Deeson with his flashlight—he has been promoted to flashlight—come walking into the laundry room. I am awake. I woke up the minute the door opened. I'm curled into a ball in the corner. In the dream, the potato is under my robe, on my chest, because I stupidly retrieved it from behind the screen. I wanted to hold the potato. A stupid, weak thing to do. Deeson and the prft motion for me to get up. I get up with my arms crossed so the potato doesn't fall out. But they know. They see the lump of the potato right away. So much weight has been lost that it sticks out. Deeson comes behind me and grabs my arms and twists them. The potato falls out. Deeson marches me out of the laundry room and down the hall. Everything is white, white, white, whiter than I remember from the last time they let me out. They're marching me down the hall to the Court of Ascendance Law. The table of Refuse from the Secular World is on the left. Hi, duct-taped hairbrush, hi, duct-taped condom, hi, duct-taped debit card, hi . . . pencil. Oh pencil. My pencil.

This dream has not come true yet, but I keep dreaming it. The dream comes and I can't stop it.

Potato eyes turn into roots that grow and grow and grow toward the light. The roots feed off the body of the potato and the green aboveground leaves, and one potato will make many more potatoes. The potato is hope. Pray for the potato.

Sesame, I am tired. I am dizzy. Sometimes I think I'm hallucinating. Sometimes voices come to me and I stop and listen carefully to figure out if the voices are real or if they're in my head. They are real when they're the prft or Deeson. They are in my head if they're you. Sometimes I hear you, Sesame, but it's not a conversation from before I began living down here. They are conversations from now. You and Inky and Sebastian are talking about how to find me. You and James One and James Two are talking about how to find me. You are talking to Peabop and Prince about how to find me.

Look for me in the city, Sesame. What city, I don't know. A city within four to six hours' driving distance from Uptown. I listed them in the beginning, in Hello Kitty.

Hello Kitty still lives and breathes dust in the dark crawl space beyond the screen vent. Hello Kitty is keeping the potato company.

Sounds of the city come through the vent. Listen to them:

The *beep beep beep* of a garbage truck backing up.

The *wheee-oh wheee-oh* of the ambulance going by.

The twirling sound of a police siren.

They are faint but they are there. I still hear them. I'm in a city.

Wait.

Every single sound that comes through these walls from the outside is a familiar sound, so familiar that I never once had to stop to think what it was. Which means am I actually here in Minneapolis? Is this where I've been all along?

We drove and we drove and we drove and the prft told us we were driving to a distant land, but was where we were driving around and around and around and around the streets of our own city? *Ye shall descend into the darkness underground, and ye shall ascend when ye have abandoned the refuse from the secular world.*

Am I here, Sesame? Is this where I am?

It is pitch-black in the laundry room. No light gives. It's not like your house, Ses, which even with all the blankets tacked to the walls is not lightproof, because of the skylight. On clear nights you can see the moon and the stars through it. On rainy nights the drops slide and puddle at the bottom. Snow drives down onto the glass or drifts down in slow, heavy flakes. The skylight can be entirely covered with snow, but it still gives light. It's never entirely dark in your house, my girl. My girl, my girl. Are you alone right now? Are you scrolling poems? Do you remember the day I told you that our bodies are 50 to 75 percent water?

"Mine's not. Mine's fifty to seventy-five percent poem."

You flashed that back at me and I laughed and you laughed but the thing is, Sesame, I believe you. Your pockets are filled with poems and many ~~was~~ is the night we ~~sat~~ sit on your bed and scroll them up and talk so soft no one, not even the rabbits up and down the alley, can hear us. I miss talking to you, Sesame. I miss hearing you quote poems.

"'A heart that laughter has made sweet, these, these remain, but I record what's gone,'" you say. "'A crowd will gather, and not know it walks the very street whereon a thing once walked that seemed a burning cloud.' Name that dead poet."

"Langston Hughes?"

"No way."

"Danez Smith?"

"Micah, get your poets straight. Danez Smith is *living*. He's like *very young*. He lives in *Saint Paul*."

"Kidding, Ses. I know who wrote that poem. It was your man Yeats."

You laugh and then flow toward me across the bed, across the poems strewn between us. It's thinking about nights like that that keeps me going. Danez Smith got it right. You are the place where ruin ends.

20

Sesame

WINTER BREAK MEANS no tutoring, which, weirdly, I miss even though it takes an hour of daylight when I could be looking for Micah. Vong and his poems, Vong and his worry, Vong who loves Micah. After I leave my daily message on Officer Emmanuel's voice mail, I put on all my layers and go straight to pick up Peabop and Prince. The Jameses are both home when I get there. It's like the whole world stops between Christmas and New Year's. People stay home.

Peabop and Prince are already waiting at the door for me, accustomed to our new walk-all-day routine. But the Jameses ask me to sit down with them on the couch for a minute, and right away I'm on guard. Do they know something? One of Micah's T-shirts is shoved down in my jacket pocket, and I put my hand over it for comfort.

"Hey," I say to the pups, and I glance up to see a troubled look on James Two's face. He puts his hand on my shoulder.

"Listen," he says. "Inky called us last night."

Instantly I'm angry. Inky was talking about me behind my back *again*?

"She told us some things that concern us about you," he says, and James One nods.

"She and Sebastian have never been to your house?" James One says. "They've never met your aunt? They don't even know where you live?"

My heart is racing. It feels as though things are crumbling around me, my carefully built life, my web of silence and omissions. I interrupt.

"You should be concerned about *Micah*," I hiss. "Why doesn't anyone believe me? Why do I have to do everything alone?"

By the time I get to the word "alone," it comes out in a whisper.

"Don't you know how scared I am?" I say. "I'm so, so scared. The officer doesn't think anything's wrong and Inky and Sebastian are angry at me and I look and look and look and—" I stop.

"My grandmother always told me to depend on myself," I tell them. "Not to ask for help. She always said I was enough for her and that she didn't need anybody else."

"But asking for help is just . . . being human," James One says.

He looks confused. Bewildered, even.

"Well, I asked for help from Officer Emmanuel," I say. "And she wouldn't even reopen the case! And I asked for help from Inky and Sebastian, and now they're starting to doubt me."

"We don't doubt you," James Two says. "At first we weren't as concerned as we maybe should have been, because there was the note, and the officer wasn't concerned, but then—"

"We realized that this is *you*," James One says, "and *Micah*. And the two of you are wiser than most adults of our acquaintance."

"So, we're coming with you," James Two says. "Until he's found or—" James One shoots him a quick look. "Until he's *found*," James Two repeats, "we're devoting ourselves to the cause. Three of us can cover more ground than one."

It's four days after Christmas and their tree is still up and presents are still under it and a holiday garland is strung up above their fireplace and the Jameses could be here, in their warm house, enjoying themselves, but no.

They believe me.

They want to help me.

That's when I break down.

"I need to tell you both something," I say.

They look at me and wait. They're normal, nice people.

They're used to telling each other things. It doesn't scare them the way it scares me. I take a deep breath.

"I live alone, okay?" I say. "I don't have an aunt, okay?"

I hate the way my voice trembles. I hate them knowing how scared I am. I hate telling my secrets. But . . . it also feels like a relief.

"Oh, Sesame G.," James One says. "Why didn't you tell us?"

"We could have helped," James Two says, and he wraps his arms around me.

I'm used to only Micah's arms around me, and before that—it feels like a long time ago now—my grandmother. James Two smells different from either of them, and he hugs me differently too. But not in a bad way. His hug feels good. It feels great. So does James One's hug, when he joins us. And again, I'm ugly crying. James One kneels beside me and rocks me back and forth. James Two brings a roll of paper towels so I can blow my nose and dry my face.

"You guys," I say. It comes out all choked. God, I hate it when my voice is like this. But the Jameses don't care.

"Listen," James One says. "There's clearly a lot to talk about here. Where do we begin? How can we help you right here and right now? First, do you want to live with us?"

"We've got room!" James Two says. "Guest bedroom with en suite bath, ready and waiting for you."

They're full of energy now, ready to leap into action and help me. But I shake my head. That's not the kind of help I want or need. Not when Micah's been missing for seventeen days.

"Thank you," I say, and my voice is back to normal. "But the only help I need right now is finding Micah."

"Got it," James Two says.

"Point us in the right direction," James One says.

They jump up, ready to go. I outline a strategy: We'll all start out together, so I can coach them. Then we'll split up. James One will cover this section of square blocks, and James Two will cover another section, and Prince and Peabop and I will cover another.

Then the Jameses put on all their layers and tie their boots in double knots, and I haul the T-shirt out of my jacket pocket and hold it under Prince's and Peabop's noses, and out into the cold we go. As we walk to our starting point, the Jameses ask about Micah—not in terms of the Prophet or the compound or the disappearance—but just about him. As if he's somewhere close by, as if none of us are worried, as if we're not out searching for him right this minute. It feels like ordinary conversation: what Micah likes to do, what our plans for the future are, things like that.

I know they're just trying to distract me, but weirdly, I start talking.

I tell them about Micah's cooking, how no one makes grilled cheese or scrambled eggs as good as he does. I tell them about the café, our possible names for it, that Micah wants a food name, like Onion. Or Potato.

"Nice," James One says. I can't tell which restaurant

name he thinks is nice, but I don't ask because I suddenly have so much to tell him about Micah.

"He loves fire," I say. "Like fire spinning, do you know what that is?" I don't wait for a response. "And wood-stoves and fireplaces. Even electric fireplaces like the one I have at my house. Oh, and the luminaria ice sculptures on Lake of the Isles in February! We were thinking of making one this year. Like, what would we make, though? What would be a good ice sculpture?"

I don't wait for them to say anything. Words are spilling out of me.

"Kids love Micah," I say. "He's one of those kid magnets, you know? Like Vong, the kid I tutor at Greenway Elementary. He met Micah once when Micah was waiting for me and it was, like, love at first sight. Vong writes him poems now. So do other people, people I don't know—they leave them in the poem boxes. Notes and poems."

"Poem boxes?" James Two says. "What are they?"

I tell them about the poem boxes, about the poems that got me through when my grandmother died, how I'm always in search of new poems. How poems are a kind of lifeline. How in the wake of Micah's disappearance I've been stocking the poem boxes with flyers, and how people have been leaving notes. The notes are different now. More urgent. *Have you called the cops? Have you talked to his school? Have you tried a psychic? Is he on opioids? Have you tried all the homeless shelters? Have you called all the hospitals?*

"I'm collecting them all on a table in the corner of my

place," I say. "I'm saving them all for when Micah comes home. That's going to be his Christmas present."

I don't tell them how hard it is to walk through the door of my house and see the poems flat and unscrolled on the table in the corner, lines and rhymes jumbling up in the still air of my still, cold house. Yeats says, *Never give all the heart* and Lucille Clifton says, *Let the rivers pour over my head* and Danez Smith says, *Let him find honey where there was once a slaughter* and then I'm crying. Again.

Is this what happens when you've never been a crier? Does all the crying you never did in the past just start coming out in a whoosh?

We stop in an alley, all of us—the Jameses, me, Peabop and Prince—and the Jameses put their arms around me again. James One hauls a travel pack of tissues out of his pocket, because of course he would have such a thing with him at all times, and James Two squeezes my shoulder and says things like, "It's going to be okay, Sesame," and "Keep the faith," and I'm trying. I'm trying to keep the faith.

The Jameses search with me and the pups all day. We text each other every hour with a meetup place to warm up, to refuel, to describe the abandoned buildings we've found and how every one of them seems to be truly abandoned. James One inspected two white passenger vans, but one was missing two out of its four tires and the other belongs to the Happy Hopper Preschool. James Two was walking by a hardware store and could have sworn he saw Micah working the cash register, but when he went inside, it was just a boy who looked like Micah.

"And not even that much like him," James Two says. "I guess I just *wanted* him to be Micah."

Tell me about it. I've seen boys like that in the last seventeen days. My heart skips a beat every time, but it's never Micah. Ghost Micahs. Mirage Micahs. Not-Micahs.

The sun goes down in the late afternoon, and the dogs are drooping and so are we. Long day. Long, long seventeen days. Another day gone. Another night dropped down on me, and the city, and Micah, wherever he is.

We walk back to the Jameses' house, and they insist that I stay with them. I shake my head.

"You have to understand," I say. "I'm not ready to talk about where I live and how I live right now. I am fine on my own."

They look doubtful.

"And you also have to understand that if Micah manages to escape, he'll come to my house," I say.

They still look doubtful. They look at each other, communicating silently, and then back at me.

"We understand," James One says. "But you're not walking home in the dark by yourself. No arguments, Sesame G."

"I'm not going home yet," I lie. "I'm meeting up with a friend at Lunds. Literally two blocks away."

"Fine," James Two says. "We'll walk you there."

"Fine," I say, and roll my eyes. But the truth is, it's

nice. It's nice to have them on either side of me, walking me down to the crosswalk, waiting with me until the light turns green. I cross and turn at the entrance to Lunds and wave. They are still there, watching to make sure I get safely inside. I wave. They wave back.

The friend line was a lie, of course. I don't let myself think about how nice it would be if it weren't a lie. What I do instead of meet up with my nonexistent friend is buy some tea and rice crackers and cheese. Then I walk out the back door and head home to lie on my bed and try to keep the panic at bay.

The thing is that people can disappear. They can die, for example. Or they can move. Or they can be sucked into a dark orbit little by little and you don't even know it's happening until *poof*, one day you go to their house and there are their phones, lined up neatly by the toaster, with a cryptic message scrawled in black on the dry-erase board.

You're going along and going along and not thinking much beyond the day by day until something shatters the day by day. And then do you know what happens? You look back and think how much you didn't appreciate while you had it.

"What are you most afraid of?" James One asked earlier.

"That he could be . . . gone."

I didn't say *lost to the cult*. I didn't say *changed forever in the hands of the Prophet*. I didn't say *dead*. But that's what I meant.

"Keep the faith," James Two said, when he was trying to comfort me.

James Two and Officer Emmanuel, both of them urging me to keep the faith, when can't they see that's all I'm doing?

I wish you were here, Micah.

The first time you stayed over was back when the Prophet was someone we laughed at. Your parents had already started going to bed early, though, on orders of the Prophet, and board-game nights were rare. It was November, my favorite month. It was snowing. Snow pattering on the tin roof, snow crunching under the car wheels, snow thunked against the side of my house by shovelers. *Thunk. Thunk. Thunk.* Every shovelful of snow made the walls shudder. Maybe the shovelers think, *It's an abandoned house, no one lives there, no one's going to notice if we just toss all the snow in front of their abandoned garage.* I do, though. I notice.

You snuck out and came over. The ice was glazing across the ruts in the alley and I could hear you coming. That's another thing that happens when you live on an alley: you hear people walking by, inches from your body. You realize over and over how little separates you from another person's body. Most people feel safe behind walls, but what are most walls but an inch of wood? Easily kicked in. Easily burned down.

Almost nothing separates us one from another, when you think about it, which most people don't. And that's how we go through the world. That's how we get through the world. There's a difference between go and get, even if it's not much of a difference.

As close to the hustle of Uptown as my house is, it's still quiet at night. Even when the bars let out late on the weekend, the suburban bros and their shrieking dates don't tend to come this way. Once in a while they do, if they're cheap and they parked on one of our side streets to avoid the parking fees. They go stumbling over the gardens and across lawns. They leave behind empty red Solo cups and cigarette butts and crushed flowers and sometimes a used condom.

You knocked on the side door. It was the softest knock—a *tap, tap, tap*—and it didn't scare me because of the softness. There was respect in the softness of that knock. Maybe you didn't want to wake me up if I was asleep. Maybe you didn't want to scare me. Maybe you were trying to let me know it was you, just by the way you knocked.

"Sesame?"

A whisper as soft as the knock. That ~~was~~ is you, Micah, not wanting anyone to see you, or me, or know that the bowing-in abandoned garage is actually a house that a girl lives in. I unlocked the door and there you were. You were smiling, and snowflakes were twirling down onto your hair. You radiated cold outdoor air, that cold fresh smell that only happens when someone who's been outside in winter comes inside. I pulled you inside and locked the door behind you and then I put my arms around you and pushed my face into your collar so I could breathe in that cold fresh air.

It was just the two of us, no parents the way there was when we were at your house, no outside world to distract us. It was you and me and the house holding us in its arms. My little bow-legged house, curving itself around us.

Warm.

Winter.

Snow.

You.

Remember?

21

Micah

QUESTION: What does it take to have seventeen people follow a single manipulative narcissist below the surface of the earth to do exactly as he says?

Answer: Seventeen people will follow a single manipulative narcissist below the surface of the earth and do exactly as he says for the same reason that a playground bully will order his minions around on the playground and everyone will do his bidding: because no one stood up to him.

"Because no one stood up to him." Seven words, one sentence.

➤ ➤ ➤

Because no one stood up to him.

Not the adults, who are supposed to know better.

Not the ones he was bullying or the ones who stood by and watched the bullying.

Not the parents, who are supposed to protect their children.

Not *my* parents, who were supposed to protect *me*.

No one stood up to him.

No one stood up to him.

No one stood up to him.

<u>*No one stood up to him.*</u>

No one stood up to him.

NO ONE FUCKING STOOD UP TO HIM

NO ONE

NO ONE

NO ONE

Not even me.

22

Sesame

IT HAS BEEN eighteen days since he disappeared. All night I had awful dreams, in which I was trying to get to Micah—I could see him across Bde Maka Ska, waving to me, calling to me, in trouble—but my legs wouldn't move. And I couldn't scream. And no one else was around. The entire city was frozen over, white, silent, while Micah kept calling and calling. When I wake up and check my phone, Inky's texted me: Sester, can you meet us? Library opens at 9.

Do they know something? Is there news? I jump out of bed and run to the library, where both Inky and Sebastian are waiting for me in the conference room. Their faces are set and serious, and my stomach turns to ice.

"Oh my God," I say. "Did you hear something?"

Inky jumps up, looking startled, and holds out her hands to me. "No, no," she says. "We haven't heard anything. I'm so sorry—I should've been clear in my text."

She tries to put her arms around me, for an Inky hug, but I sink down into a chair.

"Then what is it?" I say. "I thought you must have news."

Sebastian clears his throat. "Look, Sesame, we're sorry."

"We haven't handled things right," Inky continues. "I mean, it *is* weird that we literally don't know where you live, and then we started thinking how there's a lot we don't know about you, and after we talked to you we called the Jameses even, to compare notes, and—"

"We probably came across as angry," Sebastian interrupts. "But the thing is, we're worried about you."

"Me? It's Micah you should be worried about," I say, yet again.

I hear the tone of my voice. It's defensive and abrupt. My instant reaction is to deflect attention from me onto something else. Don't ask for help, turn away from it when offered, do everything yourself. *Be vigilant. Protect yourself.* The Jameses have offered help and I have taken it. The notes and poems in the poem boxes are a kind of silent help, and I have taken them, too.

Inky and Sebastian exchange a glance. Inky shakes her head ever so slightly. Are they silently telling each other to give up? Inky turns to me.

"Ses," she says. "We're your best friends, right?"

I say nothing. Because yes, they *are* my best friends.

But here's the thing I've been thinking about in the days since the last time we met here in the conference room, on all the nights I lie on my bed not sleeping: a lie of omission is still a lie. If your best friends don't know where you live, how well can they possibly know you? If your best friends don't know any of the particulars about where you go and what you do when you're not with them, how can they fully trust you?

Grandma, I hate to say it, but you messed up. You took good care of me, but you didn't think about the future. You didn't imagine a world where you aren't but I am. I had to figure it all out on my own, Grandma.

"Sesame?" Inky says now.

My thoughts are chasing each other and I haven't said anything and they are both looking at me. Studying me.

"Sesame?" Inky says again. "Sester?" She taps the side of her own head. "What's going on in there? What are you thinking?"

In my mind I see my grandmother in the kitchen, dicing vegetables, crimping pot stickers, playing solitaire late at night and listening to talk radio. I hear her telling me not to depend on others, not to ask for help, to rely only on yourself. This is the soundtrack of my life.

But you know what else is part of the soundtrack now? Her voice on that last day. *Don't be afraid like me.*

I just told the Jameses how scared I am, Grandma. Is this what not being afraid means?

My mind is all jumbled up. I'm so tired. I'm so scared.

"Aw, Shaolin," Sebastian says. "C'mon, talk to us." He makes his prayer hands, but slow and sad this time. Inky's eyes fill with tears.

Nothing I used to do before the disappearance—reading poems and listening to music and watching the snow fall on the skylight and talking to Micah and eating the food he made me and looking at photos of my grandmother and me and making the rounds of my poem boxes and tutoring Vong and thinking up names for Micah's and my future café, all the things that happened in my house that were routine and ordinary and beautiful and kept me sane and made me happy—matters anymore. It's like it all happened in another world. The before world.

Every day I walk out of my house into sun that splinters into shards of lightning when it reflects off the snow. It hurts my eyes. It hurts me.

My house itself hurts. What used to be my refuge isn't. What used to be a place where I slept all night long, with the stars above me through the skylight, isn't. What used to be a place I kept to myself, a place that held my secrets, a place I didn't want anyone but Micah to know about, is now a place where I'm . . . alone.

Inky pulls a cappuccino for me out of her backpack and passes it to me just as a toddler glances at the conference room's floor-to-ceiling glass windows. His eyes open wide and he shrieks, "No food or drink in the li-berry! That lady has a drink in the li-berry!" His father hushes him and Inky rolls her eyes.

"Ses," she begins, but I hold up my hand.

"Do you two want to come to my house?" I say. Their eyes open wider than the toddler's, whose cry of li-berry indignation can still be heard in the distance beyond the conference room.

"Jesus, Shaolin," Sebastian says. "How long have you lived here?"

He and Inky stand in the middle of my house, directly beneath the skylight, looking around. They're still, like they're afraid to move. Like it's a dollhouse and maybe they'll break something.

"Since a month after my grandma died."

Sebastian gapes. "Are you *serious?*"

I shrug. Yes, Sebastian, I'm serious. Inky says nothing. She looks around, her gaze traveling over all the quilted walls, the two-burner hot plate set on top of the miniature refrigerator, the recliner, my bed and its piles of more quilts, the table in the corner with all the poems waiting to be scrolled. She cranes her neck back and up, and her mouth falls open as she stares up at the skylight, which on this cloudless day is almost too bright to bear.

I try to look at it through their eyes, the eyes of people who have never seen my house. Do they hate my house?

Do they think it's ugly? Uninhabitable, even? Dark flickers of words form themselves at the base of my spine.

But Inky cranes her neck back down and looks straight at me. "You, Sester," she says, "are a mad genius."

Sebastian's head is going up and down, a lovely slow clap of a nod. He and Inky step out of the skylight's circle of light and begin to walk around, inspecting. Inky sits down in the recliner and leans back so that the footrest pops out. Sebastian runs his hand over the Amish star quilt that Micah found for me. He flicks on the electric fireplace and Inky stretches her toes out to it and smiles.

"You did this all by yourself?" Sebastian says, and I nod. "And you wonder why I call you Shaolin."

"Your grandmother never knew about this?" Inky says, and I shake my head. It's hard to talk; the now-familiar lump has risen up in my throat. Dizziness rushes up inside me and I sit down hard on the bed. The circle of light from the sun is hot on my head. My grandma never saw my house. She will never see my house.

"Do you think she would hate it?" I say.

Inky laughs, a snort that's less laugh and more surprise. "Hate it? Your grandmother would love this place."

"Anyone would love this place," Sebastian says. "You've got a future in Tiny Home design, Shaolin."

It's weird how something can change in an instant. A minute ago, I was looking around with what I thought was their eyes and seeing ugliness and dilapidation. Now I'm looking around a house that's tiny and beautiful. A house my grandmother would be proud of me for finding. A house that others want to be inside.

"Micah knows about this place?" Inky says, but then before I can nod, she answers her own question. "Of course Micah knows about this. Micah knows everything, doesn't he?"

She stands up from the recliner and walks over to the table of poems, her fingers sifting through the colored slips of paper. She holds one, then another, then another up to the light. Sebastian joins her and picks up the tall stack of notes and poems people have left in the poem boxes for Micah. He begins to read them silently, his lips moving.

"I'm saving them for Micah," I say. "His Christmas present."

Inky takes part of the stack and together they stand, reading through them. If Micah were here, he would be crouched in front of the miniature fridge or scanning the shelves, looking for ingredients, concocting a meal first in his head and then with his hands. In an hour we would be sitting together on the floor beneath the skylight, plates on laps. It's weird how sometimes the absence of a person makes them seem more present. Just then Inky looks up at me, like she's reading my mind.

"I wish I'd known your grandma," she says. "You know? Like, really known her. I wish I'd grown up going to your apartment and hanging out with you and her."

Yeah. Me too, Inky. Because you not knowing her just makes it lonelier without her. There's no one to talk about my grandma with. No one to laugh at how she used to tell me to crimp the hell out of the dumplings. No one to remember her with, her worship of Dolly Parton, her late-night solitaire games.

My how-could-you-go-and-die-on-me grandma. My do-you-know-how-awful-it-is-to-be-without-you grandma. A giant wave of missing her brings me to my knees, right there on the floor. Grandma. Then Sebastian and Inky are kneeling beside me, Inky's arms around me.

"I miss her so much," I manage at last.

"Yeah," Sebastian says, and he nods in sorrow. "You never talk about her, though. That's what we figured. Inky and me, that's one of the things we've wondered about."

Inky nods.

"Have the Jameses seen your house?" she asks, and I shake my head.

"No. Only Micah. And now you."

"Let me ask you a question, Ses. Why didn't you come live with us, after your grandmother died? You could've, you know."

I shake my head again. Inky's house is *her* house. Her parents. Her sister. Her bedroom. Everything fit together so neatly, a complete jigsaw puzzle with no missing pieces and no leftover pieces, just the way my grandmother and I fit together. At Inky's, I would have been a leftover piece. Everything would have hurt even worse than it did living alone. Correction: until Micah came along.

"Come on," I say. "We have to go. He's out there, waiting for us."

Peabop and Prince and the Jameses and I have already covered most of Whittier and Uptown and Lyndale and Linden Hills. More than two weeks into the disappearance, and amazingly, no new snow has fallen. That sometimes happens in the heart of winter. It's been so cold that none of the snow on the ground has melted. It's pristine and clean in the backyards we glimpse from the alleys. We search from the sidewalks and then retrace our steps down the alleys, the way I've been doing from the beginning.

We restaple flyers. Check the poem boxes. The nameless kid has left another note in the box at Grand and Harriet.

> I wish on the moon
> I wish on a star
> that the boy who's gone
> has not gone far.

Me too, nameless kid, me too. I pass the poem to Inky, who passes it to Sebastian, and we all nod. Then I fold the poem up and put it in my back pocket. I will take it home with me and add it to the other notes that unknown people have left in the poem boxes. The underground poetry network, watching over us.

Onward.

Today I break a limb off a buckthorn leaning onto the sidewalk from someone's buried garden—buckthorn is invasive; it's okay to hurt it—and we walk up to the sides of the abandoned buildings and swipe it along the half-buried windows. Poke it into the unused air vents, most of which are crisscrossed with ancient, linty spiderwebs.

In the parking lots, the sunlight on the untouched snow is blinding. We are walking in concentric squares, block to block, larger and larger. If we're close to a poem box, we detour so I can re-flyer it and remove the notes left inside. We scan the alleys and streets for white vans. Doesn't matter if they're passenger vans or not, we check out every single one.

"I'm up to forty-two white vans," I say. "None of them look suspicious, though. And I'm up to thirty-three abandoned buildings, not including abandoned houses. I only count buildings big enough to house a compound."

"Do you think he somehow senses that we're looking for him?" Inky says.

"I hope so."

He is somewhere not far away.

That is the thought I hold on to. Because things are bad. I can feel it. He's in bad shape. We have to find him. He is somewhere not far away.

He *is*.

He has to be.

23

Micah

I'M THINKING ABOUT embedded reporters. People who go to places like Myanmar and Kabul and Baghdad and Sudan. The front lines, where dirt and cold and danger are part of the deal. But the truth has to be told, and it can only be told if someone's in the middle of the action, seeing it with their own eyes, writing about it, photographing it.

Embedded reporters don't always make it out alive. Think about it. Maybe the names Marie Colvin and Daniel Pearl and Anthony Shadid aren't familiar to you, but guess what? They were embedded, all of them. And they're dead, all of them.

Sesame, do you remember when I told you that Walt Whitman was a war reporter? You shook your head. You frowned. You didn't want your man Whitman to be a war guy—your exact words, Sesame, *I don't want Walt Whitman to be a war guy*—but he was. He was a poet, and he was a warmonger. He contained multitudes, like in your favorite quote of his. We all do, I guess.

War reporters are out there right now. They're embedded with troops, they're freelancers on their own, they're running through the woods and the desert and the plains with cell phones and notebooks and spare batteries. War photographers are running alongside them, cameras pounding against their chests. They're dirty. They're hungry. They're tired. They're scared.

There are wars everywhere.

It takes guts to speak the truth. To stand up to the ones who don't. Guts that I thought I had but maybe don't. My points are in the deep negatives now. Wasn't I supposed to be cast out of eden right now, whatever that actually means? What starts small feeds on itself and gets bigger, and the bigger it gets the more it needs and the more it eats, which makes it get even bigger and need even more. Tumors are like that. They feed on the blood supply around them and grow fat and big. You'd think that being fat and big would be enough, wouldn't you? That they'd stop demanding so much blood at that point. But it's the exact opposite. The bigger you are, the more you demand.

The prft had some followers who believed what he said,

and then he had Deeson, who *really* believed what he said. But did Deeson, really? Or did Deeson get a taste of what power felt like and decide he wanted more? Does Deeson believe in the words of the prft, or does Deeson believe in power?

The potato is still hidden. They haven't found it.

We used to have potatoes all the time. There was a bag of them in a corner of the house I lived in with my parents, and we baked them and fried them and boiled them and roasted them with olive oil and salt. And I used to make sweet potatoes. I used to slow-roast them with ginger and butter and sea salt, so by the time you ate them they had melted into something soft and sweet and so delicious. Remember, Ses?

In the end, it's not about the end. It's not about surviving the end of days and the destruction and mayhem and war that will happen in them. It's not about learning how to cope with the rigors of modern-day life. It's not about ascending to the next world on a beam of light or a shining spaceship or however you hear it described. I don't know what it's about, but it's not about that.

They will be outside the laundry room door soon, listening. Deeson and the prft. I will hear their robes brushing. I will hear them laughing. Soon they will call my name the way they've begun to call it. Soon they will tell me that my parents have disowned me, abandoned me, given up on me. Soon they will ask me if I'm ready to go.

They are trying to make me lose my mind. *Are you ready to go yet, Micah? Are you ready to go? Ready to go?*

Fuck them.

I'm not going down that easy.

When I haul myself onto the top of the laundry tub, I have to crouch there for a minute. Stars flicker in the darkness. Are they in my head or are they in the air? It's so lightless in the laundry room that you can't tell what's inside or outside. Cool thick cloth brushes my head. A robe. It's easy to forget that above my head are robes, hanging side by side. A basement choir missing its human bodies, which are down the hall in the Room of Reflection, murmuring. Bless the child. Thoughts and prayers.

Dizzy.

Do this, Micah. Reach up from the laundry tub and feel for the screen.

Nothing. Only air. Lose your balance and tumble back and down, into the laundry tub itself. It feels good, doesn't it? Four walls rising up around you. Small and confined. Only your head is higher than the walls. Only your head is exposed in the cold air where stars aren't flickering anymore.

Keep going.

Get to your knees in the laundry tub. Four thick tub walls still strong around you. Reach up and out with both hands and feel through the air. Robes, stiff and still. Where's the screen? *You have to stand up, Micah.* Micah has to stand up. Micah stands up. Micah is dizzy. The four strong walls are far below now. Micah stands in the darkness and feels around him with both hands. Which way is he facing now? He doesn't know. Turn around, Micah. Keep turning, keep reaching. You will feel the screen sooner or later.

Sooner! The murmuring down the hall is suddenly less faint. The door of the Room of Reflection must have opened and the Bless the Child choir is in the hall now. Someone might come unlock the laundry room, and if that happens, they will see you in the laundry tub and know you're up to no good.

"What are you doing, Micah?"

"Nothing."

"What are you doing, Micah?"

"Nothing."

"What are you doing, Micah?"

"Fuck you."

Be quick. Focus. The air in front of you is different. Denser. The existence of a cement wall creates a barrier that changes the quality of the air before it. Push your hand through the dense air. Wiggle it. Search.

Screen.

Feel with your fingertips for the scratched-out place at the bottom right. Dig in and pull. Keep pulling until the whole screen gives way into your hands. In the dark, lower it into the laundry tub.

Now balance on the upper edge of the tub. This is a

leap of faith. You have only one chance. Crouch and then spring up and forward with both arms stretched out.

BANG.

That was your head against the top of the opening. Oh Jesus oh Jesus oh Jesus it hurts, but you're in the black crawl space and you're sweeping your hands back and forth through the dust and dirt and chunks of rock and broken-off cement and deadness that's in here. The air is dust and grit and stale and harsh. You start to cough but you hold it in because the others are out there. And you can't let them hear you. Your body shakes and explodes silently with silent coughs.

There.

The notebook. Hello Kitty. Hello, Kitty.

And the potato. Solid, colder than my cold hands, but still there.

This is where you'll move forward on your knees with Hello Kitty and the potato in your hands. You'll keep your head down. You'll want to rub the top of it where you feel the bruise rising and the blood trickling, but you won't.

Think of the embedded reporters, whose mission it is to report what's really happening to the outside world. Keep moving forward. You'll open your eyes in the stale cramped blackness and sweep them back and forth. You'll see nothing. You'll see nothing. You'll see nothing. Then you'll see . . . something. Not *something*, but not-black. You'll keep inching forward toward the not-black.

When you get to the not-black, you will see that it's the

opening to some kind of tube. A vent? A tunnel? Inches across. The not-blackness is because the tunnel gives onto the outside world. It does. It has to.

Your hands are shaking. Clench the potato between your teeth so that your hands are free to twist Hello Kitty and roll her into a tube. As small a tube as they can. The potato is heavy between your teeth. It has been so long since you ate anything. You squint and shake your head and try to see, try to see, try to see. Oh my God let me see. Please let me see. But the only thing to see is not-blackness. Beyond that, nothing.

You have one chance and you take it. You crouch at the base of the not-blackness and hold the roll of Hello Kitty in one hand and push the potato as far as you can into the tunnel with the other. When you can't push it any farther, you push Hello Kitty in after it. You push and push and push through dirt and cobwebs until your arm is as far as it can go and almost stuck in the tunnel. Then you pull it back through and swipe your fingers against your robe to get the cobwebs off. Then you back your way up to the opening of the crawl space. Drop yourself back down. Find the tub in the darkness, through the hanging silent robes. Find the screen. Maneuver it back into the yawning space. Make it fit.

Go back to the corner and huddle into it, into the crook between the two walls. Breathe in your own sweat and filth and stench. The prickles of hair on your head are matted with sweat and blood. The bump on top of your head is egg-like.

Somewhere in the not-darkness beyond the tunnel a siren wails.

Think your way through various scenarios. When they come for you, what will you do? Will you fight? Will you scream? Will you call for help from the minions who surround Deeson and the prft? Will you remind them of the better angels of their nature? Will you remind them of how things used to be in the world you all came from? Have they already forgotten? It doesn't take long. It takes far less time than you'd think. In the very end, the very last seconds, will you scream for your parents?

When they come for you, what will *they* do?

After they do what they will do, what will happen to the others?

Will a day come, after winter has passed, that the stench from the basement of an abandoned building disturbs whoever walks by? Will that disturbed passerby call 3-1-1 to report the smell? Will a couple of cops break down the door and discover the rotting corpses of sixteen followers, one rebel, and a man who called himself the Prophet? Will the *Star Tribune* report the discovery on the front page? Will your friends remember you as Micah, who descended below the earth as a war correspondent? Or just as Micah, who descended?

Journalists die in the line of work. They die trying to make the truth of the matter known. But if you die down here, you will have died without making the truth known to the outside world.

Dearly beloved, we are gathered here in the laundry room to witness the trial of Minor Micah Stone, traitor to the people. Despite our best efforts at forgiveness and rehabilitation, Minor Stone has proved recalcitrant and resistant to all our attempts. Moreover, he has placed the lives of the people at risk. Whatsoever he hath done to us, let us do to him. Shear his hair in front of the crowd that they might jeer. Remove light and sustenance and force him to live in darkness until the way is revealed to him. Micah Stone: refuse from the secular world.

24

Sesame

IT'S EARLY AFTERNOON and Inky and Sebastian and I are cold and tired and hungry and so are the dogs. We stop at Tilia—we've made it that far down into Linden Hills—and they let us bring the pups in, and then my favorite server, the one with the bird-of-paradise flower tattoo bursting up from her shoulder into the hollow of her throat, pours them a bowl of water and crumbles some rice and baked sweet potatoes into another bowl for them. They share. This is not typical for Prince and Pea-bop, but nothing is typical anymore. I haul three T-shirts out of my backpack: the Replacements, Doomtree, and Brother Ali.

"Take another hit off these shirts," I tell the dogs, and they do. I rub the shirts over their necks and backs and haunches and heads. Then I wrap one around each of their leashes, like a bandanna, and tie it below their muzzles. This way the scent of Micah will stay with them.

"Back at it," I say, once we've all sat for a minute and used the bathroom and are warmed up. The server hands us each a fish taco torta—Tilia's fish taco torta was once voted one of the Best Sandwiches in the United States, and Micah and I ~~wanted~~ *want* to have a fish sandwich on the menu at our nameless café—and out into the bright white snow we go. Again.

Inky and Sebastian link arms with me for a minute and press their heads against mine. A silent pregame almost-prayer.

Hope is not fading. Hope did not fade. Hope will not fade. We are staying in the present tense with hope because there is no other choice.

We are in Linden Hills and passing the Church of Faith, Hope, and Charity, which has been abandoned for years now. Time to run the buckthorn stick along the base-ment windows. Time to poke the dryer vent. A couple of the stained-glass windows on the side wall are cracked and broken. Pieces missing. It's weird what you notice when you get up close to abandonment. But first, check the parking lot. Scan it for signs of footsteps on the old, icy, still-pristine snow. Look for a white van. Usually there is nothing but snow and once in a while a random garbage can or broken piece of furniture, like lots of abandoned buildings—but look anyway.

The dogs are trotting behind me. Patient pups. It's time to think about getting them home. Time to gear up again for tomorrow. Hope is not fading. Hope cannot fade. We have to keep going. Sebastian and Inky have fanned out around the other sides of the church. They are looking for footprints too. They are looking for a van.

No vans on this side of the building. No footprints. I start moving across the unbroken snow, stick in hand. Then the pups surge forward on their leashes, barking. At the same time, Sebastian's voice yells from around the corner.

"Sesame! Sesame! *VAN!*"

What?

His voice sounds different. It's loud and urgent. Now he comes flying around the side of the church, Inky right behind him. They're both shouting. I let go of the leashes and the dogs head straight toward the vent on the side of the building.

"Van! Got hockey! Van!"

Jesus! I can't think. I can't breathe. A GOT HOCKEY van? My body takes over and I'm following the pups, running, running toward the vent poking out of what must be the basement. He is somewhere not far away. He is in bad shape. I can feel it. I can FEEL it. We are coming for you, Micah. We are not giving up, Inky and Sebastian and I. We reach the vent at the same time.

Prince is barking madly. Peabop next to him pushes her head forward and freezes. They are on either side of the vent. Old and rusty and half-caved-in.

They're both barking now. Urgent barks, focused and constant. I recoil when I see something brownish protruding from the vent, partly covered in snow—a dead rat? Squirrel?

Wait. No.

It's a potato.

A long, smooth, brown potato.

"Potatoes," Micah said, the day I met him, the day he was holding the Lunds bag in his arms and I asked him what was in there.

Wild hope swarms up inside me. I drop to my knees by the vent and pull the potato out, and then poke the buckthorn stick in with caution. Right away it hits something. The dogs are barking and barking. Sebastian and Inky are crouching beside me, trying to see inside. I pull off my mitten and stick my fingers in, then my whole hand, and touch the edge of something. A book? No. Paper. I can barely reach it, but I pincer my pointer and middle fingers around it and tug. And tug again. Finally it's close enough that I can grab it with my thumb and index finger and pull.

Hello Kitty.

I can't breathe.

"Oh my God!" Inky says, and "Hello Kitty?" Sebastian says. The dogs stop barking and stand there panting.

But I can't say anything, because I'm not breathing.

ALISON McGHEE

This is Micah's notebook. I can't breathe. I can't talk. It's Micah. He's in there.

"MICAH!" I scream into the vent. "MICAH! MICAH!"

From far inside the building I hear a thud. Another thud. From across the abandoned parking lot of the abandoned church there are lights and a siren. More lights, more sirens. Someone's reported us. Cops can be dangerous and they can also be good. I jump up and wave my arms so they can see I'm not carrying anything. Inky and Sebastian stand up with their arms over their heads for the same reason. People are coming out of their houses. They stand uncertainly on their steps.

"Help!" I yell. "Please help us!"

At that, the onlookers begin to move. Jacketless, mittenless, they jump off their steps and down to the sidewalk, crossing the street, flooding across the parking lot to where we stand with Hello Kitty, calling for help.

25

Micah

WHEN THE BARKING begins, you will be asleep. You will startle awake and listen. You won't believe at first that it's barking because it sounds close. Far away there will be voices. The voices will be calling a name you recognize. You will close your eyes the better to concentrate, the better to hear. The barking will intensify. The voices will get louder.

Then there will be pounding.

They will break in the door of the laundry room. Light. Harsh. Blinding.

What have you done you son of a bitch what have you done

> > >

Dogs that bark.
   Light that blinds.
   Potato that withers.
   Voices that shout.
   Cement that's cold.

26

Sesame

WHEN YOU COME back from a different world, even if that different world is somewhere not far away, you are not the person you used to be.

The boy who walked out the front door into a December night in a Minneapolis winter and got into a van that drove for hours and hours and hours in a widening, then tightening spiral no longer exists. The person who's here now has a shorn head but the same dark eyes and the same careful, quick hands. But he knows things he didn't know before. And he is changed.

The girl who woke up in her house the next morning and knew that something was wrong, the girl who set forth in the cold to find out what that wrong was and set it right, no longer exists either. She knows things she didn't know before. And she is changed.

If you ask the boy what happened, he will tell you he isn't entirely sure. That he goes over and over it in his mind. That a man set out to gain power over his fellow human beings and he did. It began slowly, with a knock on a door and an opening of that door. It began with trust and willingness on one side and a need for dominion on the other. Trust and willingness deepened into fear and subservience, and the man who wanted power gained more of it. He gained so much of it that he led his followers into an underground prison where they turned quiet and still and scared. Where they went along day by day thinking that it would end. That it would have to end.

And no one called him out. No one but the boy even questioned him.

That's something that he thinks about, now that he's aboveground again, staying with the Jameses until he's back to full health. Sometimes he has bad dreams, dreams about Deeson, or the prft, or the white scared faces of the Living Lights as they were led silently up the stairs one by one. The Jameses tell him that Ronald Gasberger is awaiting trial on several counts. The Jameses tell him that it may take some time, but his parents will be all right, and so will the rest of the followers. That he, Micah, must keep the faith. He thinks about that, about what *keeping the faith* means. He'll be thinking about that one for a long time.

A stack of notes and poems is on the table next to him. He reads through them every day, these notes from people who don't know him but who were thinking about him anyway. Who were hoping the best for him. Who were on the lookout for him.

If you ask the girl what happened, she will tell you that she isn't entirely sure either. That she goes back in time to before it happened, when she lived alone in a house that no one but the boy knew about. When, in the wake of her grandmother's sudden death, what she wanted more than anything was to make her own life. She thinks now about how terrified she was, how it was unbearable that her grandmother was gone. She thinks now that maybe what she wanted was to preserve the life she had with her grandmother, to keep it in a bubble that nothing else would touch. Now the girl knows that it's not possible to keep anything the same. That things always change. Now she sees that trying to stop the world—her own small world or the world outside—from changing is an impossible task.

She sees now that some things *should* change. She sees that even though she loved her grandmother with all her heart, her grandmother was wrong about some things, like relying only on yourself. That at the very end of her life, her grandmother knew this, and regretted it. Sesame tells herself not to be afraid. She tells herself to be fearless. To crimp the hell out of things.

It will be a while before Micah is cooking again. A while before he's back at school, back in his house, back at it, with "it" meaning the rest of his life. Maybe he won't go back to Southwest. Maybe he'll finish up at New World Online Academy. Maybe he won't move back in with his parents.

Inky and Sebastian check in about Micah. They ask me how he is, but not every day. They know that patience is key, with both him and me. As if he's tuning in to my thoughts, Sebastian looks up from the poems table. He and Inky are scrolling them up now, wrapping a rubber band around each.

"By the way, Ms. Gray, how are you and Mr. Stone doing with a name for your café-to-be?" he says.

He tilts his head like he's a CNN reporter waiting for an answer.

And somehow that makes the lump in my throat dissolve. Because Sebastian knows what he's doing by asking me that particular question, and so does Inky, and so do I. What he's saying is that someday, everything will be okay again.

Now the table is strewn with scrolled poems. Inky and Sebastian are snapping rubber bands at each other. Micah is at the Jameses' house, sleeping and eating and gaining weight while Peabop and Prince and James One and James Two watch over him. Later I will be there too, sitting beside him on the couch, maybe watching a movie, maybe reading, maybe holding his hand.

Meanwhile, it is time to refill the poem boxes. Inky and Sebastian and I fill our pockets with poems and walk out into the sunlit snow.

■ ■ ■

Acknowledgments

I'm so grateful for the support of many as I wrote this novel—first and foremost, Caitlyn Dlouhy, who helped wrangle it into shape over several drafts with her keen, kind, and perspicacious powers of editing. My thanks to Sonia Chaghatzbanian, who never fails to astonish me with the perfection of her book designs. To Valerie Shea and Jeannie Ng, sharp-eyed copyeditors who manage to see in a way I can't, to Elizabeth Blake-Linn for her production wizardry, and to Alex Borbolla for her insightful reading and all-around help—my deep thanks. My gratitude, always, to the entire wonderful team at Atheneum.

Sara Crowe, wonderful agent and beautiful person,

thank you for everything you do. More thanks to poet and dear friend Aria Dominguez, whose reaction to an early draft buoyed me through several enormous revisions. Thanks also to the police officers and social workers who took the time to help me with some of the details of the novel. Thank you to dear friends, Tom Clemens and Kelly Krebs, who were my inspiration for the Jameses. Thanks to my South Minneapolis neighborhood, the people, architecture, and landmarks of which form the foundation of Sesame's and Micah's lives.

Profound thanks to all the poets who, beginning when I was a little girl, have sustained my spirit and saved my life with their beautiful words. And finally, to all the young people speaking truth to power in terms of climate crisis, gun violence, conspiracy theories, racism and sexism and all the other isms that lessen us as humans, I cheer you on. Young activists, I see you, I hear you, and I admire your voices, steady work, and refusal to be cowed.

ALISON MCGHEE
is a *New York Times* bestselling author,
Pulitzer Prize nominee, and Christopher
Award winner who has written a slew of
critically acclaimed teen and middle-grade
novels and picture books, including *What
I Leave Behind*, *Dear Sister*, *Someday*, *Pablo
and Birdy*, *Maybe a Fox*, and *Little Boy*,
as well as several adult novels, including
Shadow Baby and *The Opposite of Fate*.
She splits her time between Minneapolis,
Minnesota, and Laguna Beach, California.
You can visit her at alisonmcghee.com.